Also by Rae Earl:

OMG! I'm In Love With a Geek!
OMG! Is This Actually My Life?

#HELP my CAT'S a VLOGGING SUPERSTAR!

Rae Earl

WALKER
BOOKS

First published in Great Britain 2017 by Walker Books Ltd
87 Vauxhall Walk, London SE11 5HJ

2 4 6 8 10 9 7 5 3 1

Text © 2017 Rae Earl
Cover design by Walker Books Ltd
Cute modern cat in blue glasses © 2016 Volantherist / Getty Images
Portrait of tabby kitten, *Felis silvestris catus* © 2016 Westend61 / Getty Images
Portrait of a cat © 2016 DRB Images LLC / Getty Images
Jumping cat © 2016 Akimasa Harada / Getty Images

This book has been typeset in Bembo, B o k k a , Avenir, Dina's Handwriting and Courier

Printed and bound in Great Britain by Clays Ltd, St Ives Plc

British Library Cataloguing in Publication Data:
a catalogue record for this book is available from the British Library

ISBN 978-1-4063-6797-3

www.walker.co.uk

#ROBOTWARS

You know you've had a bad Saturday when your cat is sulking and trying to eat your shoe at the same time. My pet hates me. My phone hates me. My mum's boyfriend hates me.

Things are looking bad right now. But before YOU start hating on me too, let me try and explain what really happened this afternoon.

Firstly, I am NOT a murderer. I did not try and kill a machine. It was just a simple misunderstanding between a very angry feline, a desk and my foot. But it's all got completely out of hand and the situation is being exploited by Mr Neat Freak and his zombie pack of dusters.

And I don't want to blame anyone for the accident, but it WAS Mum's fault. She wanted me to spend the afternoon doing my homework and had turned the Wi-Fi off. I KNOW. So I was forced to find a desperate way to get signal so I could send a message to Lauren. It was an important message that would cheer the gorgeous Laurenmeister up. A best friend who is very fed up and in need of some love.

And it should be a simple thing to message your friends. It's a human right. It is not in this house. This is a mobile black spot. Not this area. Just my house.

To try and get my message to send I had to hang out of the window with my arm waving in the air. That didn't work. Our neighbour thought I wanted to speak to her. *There is no problem, Mrs Milner. I am just living with two unreasonable control dictators.* Then I used the shower in the bathroom as a massive aerial thing. This also failed. The shower is for washing. The shower knew it was not a phone mast and would not play along.

Instead, I used my cat, Dave, as a mobile roaming device. I learnt some valuable lessons here. A phone will not balance on a cat's back, and the cat will then try and eat the phone in anger. Then try to eat the contents of your wardrobe.

Once Dave had deserted me for my socks, I had no choice but to stand on top of my desk, flex my leg and point my toes and hold my phone up in the air as high as I could. Getting a decent signal to text your best friend should NOT involve ballet, but it was worth trying for Lauren. I was pirouetting by my laptop when Dave decided she wanted to get involved. There was a huge feline leap with full claw extension onto my knee. I lost my balance and fell off the desk. My heel planted itself firmly on my mum's boyfriend's best friend.

His robot vacuum cleaner. It had come into my bedroom for a feed of dust.

As I landed on the machine, it beeped in distress. It stopped eating dirt and switched to a random programme of confusion. Dave then attempted to kill the robot vacuum cleaner by jumping on top of it. It did sort of look like an out-of-control pigeon.

At that moment, the neat freak boyfriend rushes into my bedroom and sees MY cat surfing on top of HIS robot vacuum cleaner. The Neat Freak yells at Dave, then yells at me that I've had it in for him and his "superior cleaning methods" for ages!

He then starts nursing his best friend like it's a massive soppy Labrador, reassuring it that it will all be OK. He takes it downstairs, muttering about its delicate micro-brush technology, and I haven't seen him since.

So me and Dave are now sitting in my bedroom. I still haven't managed to text Lauren and I think I am in big trouble. Which doesn't seem fair, because I've tried to get on with this man. He's my mum's boyfriend and a neat freak but I've tried. That's me, I suppose. I try to get on with everyone because things are just easier that way, aren't they? But you cannot live with a man who puts his relationship with a cleaning device before his relationship with living things.

He's even given the robot vacuum cleaner a name – McWhirter.

And McWhirter follows me everywhere. He's like my rotating, sucking-everything-up shadow. When I eat my toast at breakfast, you hear the Neat Freak saying, "There, boy! Get Millie's crumbs!" When I eat dinner, he's at his master's side. Sitting. Waiting. Staring. I know he's just a machine, but his on/off switches look like eyes. Glowing, red eyes full of tidy, hungry for a treat of some of my mess. McWhirter the cleaning robot dog has become my bossy, buzzing stepbrother. He is terrorizing me with his automatic settings and full-view sensor.

He? I'm calling McWhirter "he" now! I can't stay here. I'll go mad. I'll start talking to the dishwasher. Neat Freak does that too.

He hasn't given it a name yet but it's only a matter of time. He congratulates it when it's finished a cycle.

It's not normal, is it?

All this non-stop trauma over stupid stuff like fluffy balls on wood floors makes me think…

It makes me think I need to go and live with my dad.

I know that sounds a bit "Drama Queen". But I don't seem to belong here any more. Maybe if I just moved out for a time, Mum might miss me and realize I'm actually nice to have around. And one great thing about having parents who don't live together is that I actually have somewhere else I could go.

It's telling Mum that is going to be SO hard.

My mum isn't evil, but she's strict and tough beyond the belief of any normal human being or even a parent. Living with her is a bit like being in the army without having to wear camouflage trousers or getting the opportunity to squash people you don't like with a tank.

And yes, when I say that, I am thinking of rolling over her boyfriend. And McWhirter.

When it was just me and Mum, we slotted together more. I could cope with her rules. Obviously, her turning off the Wi-Fi at eight EVERY night apart from Saturday wasn't great, but we were at least partners in crime – or "grime" as the Neat Freak called it when he first arrived with his stupid Lycra shorts and power mop. No, Mum didn't clean much and there was an inch of furry-based mess on the top of the widescreen – but who cares?

She works at the hospital. She's not a surgeon or anything, but she has to order all the swabs and bandages. She's basically responsible for stopping people from bleeding to death on a global scale. She saves lives! She doesn't need to DUST. And she isn't keen on me cleaning too much either. She doesn't want me to become a domestic slave tied to an oven baking my signature-style Black Forest gateau for some man. She would much rather I came with her to her boxercise class or was doing my homework or BOTH. At the same time. Mum does multi-skilling like no other women dare.

I haven't got a signature-style cake by the way – mainly because Mum and me aren't big on baking. Mum says if you can get a perfectly decent apple turnover from the supermarket, why would you bother spending two hours making one? Just watch them do it on TV. I agree. We agree on most things. Or we did until Gary turned up and hoovered all of our love away.

Gary. Gary "Neat Freak" Woolton.

Do you know that only twenty-three babies in the WHOLE of this country have been called Gary in the past two years?! This is because Garys CAUSE TROUBLE. And they polish everything at the same time.

Every Friday me and Mum used to slum it together on the sofa in our pyjamas and watch a box set till one in the morning. Now Friday night for me is YouTube on my own, and Friday night for her is date night with a man who smells like Cillit Bang. I can't even watch Netflix as they're too busy watching something about the Tudors. He's ruined everything.

Since we've been back at school, Mum's insisting I start following a strict homework timetable. And don't even get me started on Gary's cleaning rota. The oven does not need cleaning daily. Before he came along, we hardly used it.

I have to get out of here. Especially now Gary thinks I'm a robot vacuum cleaner murderer. It's for Dave's protection as much as mine. Even if it's just for a few months. That's all. Nothing too drastic.

I need to think about how to tell Mum that I want to go and live at Dad's, though. But my phone is beeping like mad. Finally, I've got signal. Oh. It's Lauren.

Oh no.

No. No. NO!

It's…

This isn't good. Oh prawning HELL.

I need to get round there. Trust me. This is bad. BAD. Everything about me can wait. Lauren is in TROUBLE. THIS could go viral.

#STYLESHAMED

Lauren's mum lets me straight in. She likes me. She thinks I'm a "good influence". This is because I make Lauren live on Planet Earth for at least some part of the day. The rest of the time, Lauren is on Planet Lauren. It's a fantastic place to be, but lots of adults seem to struggle with it. I love it though. She's the opposite of me. She does, THEN she thinks.

There's no sign of Lauren's dad, which is probably why her mum is looking so cheerful. Lauren's parents don't get on. They're a soap without the funny bits.

When I get to Lauren's bedroom, she's under her duvet like a very shy and sad quilted tortoise. I can hear her sniffling.

"Go away," she moans, until she realizes it's me.

She pokes her head out. "Oh, Mills – it was just terrible. Unbelievable. Remember those new heels? My first proper pair? You said…"

I know what I said. I tried them on too and I said they should come with crutches as breaking your ankle was almost guaranteed.

"Oh no, Lauren. Have you hurt yourself?" I say to her. "They

13

are hard, Lauren. It's like balancing on really drunk giraffes. The struggle is REAL."

"I know. So I thought I'd practise just by walking to the shop. It's only three minutes away in normal shoes. Actually, it was more like twenty in these heels, but … I was doing OK until I had to go up the kerb, and then..." Lauren pops back into her blanket shell. "I heard giggling. I think someone might have been –" Lauren gulps – "following me. What if it's Mr Style Shame?"

The Mr Style Shame Instagram account has a massive number of followers. We don't know who runs it, but he's a big name round here. His logo is the outline of a guy wearing dark glasses. He's probably some Batman genius who lives in a bitter den of sass. People WE KNOW have been featured by him. He is constantly on the prowl, like a fashion lion, hunting for people who aren't looking their best. THEN he pounces. And his attacks are FATAL. He blurs your face, but everyone at school still knows who you are, and no – the adults can't stop him. They've got NO idea. They think life begins and ends with Facebook.

If you're unlucky enough to be featured, there's a very good chance you could be an online sensation nightmare in under an hour.

And now he may have a photo of my beautiful best friend tripping over in a pair of pink stilettos while carrying a can of Sprite and a Kit Kat. You see what I mean? This isn't good. And Lauren knows it.

"Have a look for me, Mills. See if I'm on there."

I pick up my phone and yes, of course I follow Mr Style Shame. Don't hate me. We all do. You need to check to make sure you're not on there. He can strike at any time and…

Yes. Sure enough, there is a photo of my beautiful best friend in mid-air with a filter to maximize her completely wonky going-all-over-the-place body. One very pink high heel is in the gutter. The other one is flying beside Lauren's shoulder like a very embarrassed parrot.

If the photo wasn't bad enough, he's written:

Look at this modern-day Cinderella leaving her crystal slippers behind! Remember if you're going for #glam, practise first, girls, or you're very unlikely to find your own Prince Charming #fail #heels #MrStyleShame

"Is it there?" Lauren whispers.

"Er … yes."

"How many likes?"

Do I lie?

I take several hundred likes off the actual figure.

Lauren pulls the duvet so far over her she looks like she may be planning to hibernate for ever. I think she's trying really hard not to cry. Her face collapses when she's upset and she doesn't want me to see. When she sobs, I sob. That's how we are.

I hate this. Lauren is my BFF. One of the sweetest, loveliest people you will ever, EVER meet. And Mr Style Shame makes so many people feel totally, trollingly BLURGH about themselves. He does that CLASSIC evil thing of pretending to be funny so he can get away with it. I'm sick of him.

But right now, I need to work out a way to make my best friend feel better.

And I think I have an idea.

#BEAREYES

If there are two things my best friend loves it's make-up and our favourite vloggers. We both do. Vlogging just cheers you up, doesn't it? And our faves are ALWAYS there – daytime or 2 a.m. when you can't sleep because you've got something on your mind.

"Come on, Lozza." I can feel her sobbing under the duvet. "He'll find a new victim in the next five minutes. You'll be forgotten by Monday."

I don't actually believe that but I just want to make her feel better. People are still talking about Holly Graham's skirt-tucked-in-her-striped-pants Mr Style Shame tragedy, but Lauren doesn't need to hear that right now.

"Let's watch Bella Fruity – the inexpensive beauty – and do some serious eyes."

Bella is one of our top vloggers. She does SERIOUSLY low-budget but highly magnificent makeovers. We have nearly worn YouTube out watching her genius with eyes. We've tried her exotic-bird look, her Cara brows, her Kardashian contouring AND her Kate Middleton wedding make-up tutorials. After that, we could have basically married Prince William. We looked brideliciously fabulous.

Today, though, I think we should keep it simple, so I say to Lauren: "Let's do Bella's perfecto winged eyeliner cat look."

Lauren finally comes out of her covers and we do our make-up. She puts hers on brilliantly but just to make her laugh, I get hold of the foundation and liquid eyeliner, pick up my phone and hit record.

"OK. So today we are going for the Panda Look. A lot of you contact me and you say, Millie, I want to look like a big furry bear in a zoo. So what do you do?! It's EASY. First of all, just get some foundation that's about five shades lighter than what you actually are. SMEAR it all over your face and then get some black liquid eyeliner and draw MASSIVE BLACK CIRCLES ALL OVER YOUR EYES. Now just grab a pot plant or some broccoli from the fridge, stick it in your mouth and – BINGO! – you're a panda! NOW, EAT THAT, BELLA FRUITY. I'm THE BIG BEAR PANDA BEAUTY! I could go to any party at any zoo in the world."

Lauren is howling with laughter behind me.

"Who cares what you look like?! Who cares if you trip over? If your BFF is upset because she thinks someone has caught her looking stupid, just do something completely spoon like this to remind her that none of us are perfect. Also, there is no shame in trying something new but there is shame in making people or bears feel bad about themselves. So THANK YOU."

I'm on an emergency goofball mission here. And it has worked. Lauren is laughing like crazy. I look crazy too. A crazy panda.

But going full spoon to cheer up Lauren is totally fine.

"Now I'm going to upload that. No one will care about your trip if they see THIS!"

I'd never normally do anything like this. Most things I share online are thought about and put through a really good filter and have been taken at least thirty times. BUT, as Aunty Teresa says, desperate times call for desperate measures. My BFF needs the love.

And I do it! To be honest, I've got hardly any views on any of my stuff, so I don't think anyone will see it. Also, I'm not sure it's going to stop people talking about Lauren's spectacular fall, but it's worth doing it to show her I'm WITH her. You'd be the same. I don't mind doing really silly stuff if *I'm* in actual control of it.

Then Lauren says something really lovely. "You always cheer me up, Mills. You always know what to do."

I sometimes do. I'm good at sorting out things for other people. Like Lauren and Aunty Teresa. What I'm not so good at is sorting out my own life. Like how to tell Mum I want to go and live with my dad because her boyfriend is the most annoying person on this earth.

"Millie," says Lauren. "Thank you. But do you want to take your panda make-up off now? It's quite difficult to take pandas seriously."

She's right. Pandas are not good at discussing who they would like to live with, as they mainly live in zoos with one partner. In fact, pandas are very lucky when you think about it. I bet no one comes in and cleans up their bamboo with a portable Dustbuster, GARY.

"You're right, Loz. I need to look the business. Dave tried to kill McWhirter and I've had enough. I'm going to tell Mum that I want to go and live with Dad for a bit."

Lauren looks taken aback. "Millie! Why do you want to leave your mum?! You two are like sisters really. But sisters that get on! I know the Neat Freak is a bit—"

This makes me cross. "Gary is not 'a bit' anything. He is a FULL-ON pain. And Mum obviously doesn't want me there, unless I'm doing school stuff. It would only be for a little while…"

Lauren looks at me and then softly says, "Millie, are you sure you're not just being a little … jealous and spoilt and only-child? Your mum deserves to be—"

I lose it slightly. "Lauren, this isn't about Mum being happy. It's about her deciding that a man who uses hospital-grade hand sanitizer as shower gel is the ONE."

Lauren backs down and changes the subject.

"By the way —" she has wrapped her duvet round herself now like some kind of very warm poncho — "have you seen the new boy?"

Have I seen the new boy? Yes, of course I have. New people at school are interesting. We know Reuben Stubbs can still fold himself up into a locker. It used to be impressive but we've seen the same trick a hundred times now. Anyone NEW is a very good thing.

Lauren looks very proud of herself. "I have information on the man!" She attempts a swagger. "He's called Danny Trudeau and he is Canadian."

"Ohhh…" I put on our MAJOR GOSSIP ALERT voice. "Is he? How has HE ended up HERE?"

Lauren starts to whisper. "Well. The rumour is that he could be related to —" Lauren looks around to check that there aren't any other people listening — "the President."

"The president of what?" I ask her. It sounds like a film.

"I don't know," Lauren says before realizing she sounds ever so slightly ridiculous and crumpling into a giggly mess on the floor.

"LOZZA!" I throw a hamburger pillow at her.

Lauren gets up and angrily slams the hamburger down so hard on the bed it loses its bun. "Now guess who is already following him on Instagram?"

We both know. Erin Breeler. How to explain her?

Erin Breeler is the Queen of Instagram at school. She is guaranteed hundreds of likes with everything she posts. She could put a pic up of her avocado salad and get total adoration from every breathing thing on this earth. Even non-breathing things like the avocados would probably like her posts.

On her account, she has the most perfect photos of her totally amazing, glowing life. Selfies like you've never seen. Her angles are perfect. Her eyebrows are sculpted. HER BUM IS A CELEBRITY ON ITS OWN. She smiles with perfect teeth (even when she had braces, she looked unbelievable) and wears clothes that the rest of us don't dare to. She does yoga poses in dungarees. It looks GREAT. You think I'm exaggerating? Go and look. The girl is phenomenal.

And even though it's all about what she looks like on the outside, she writes stuff like **Feel the inner glow radiate out** and **I can be more mindful in this mohair cardigan**, so you can't even call her shallow.

She's really clever about what she posts. When she had a spot, she made it into a good thing. She put her little finger over it, puckered her lips and posed with a **No apologies! No one is perfect!** caption. She acts like she doesn't really know what she's doing and everybody falls for it. It's so FALSE but everyone seems to love her.

Girls like Erin don't hang around with girls like me and Lauren. She's too cool. Too edgy. And if you get in her space, she will take you down in SUCH a whip-smart way. YET a weird part of me still wants her to like me.

I know – pathetic. And, honestly, I'm scared of her. And I hate that in myself. She's super confident both at school and in her posts and it's like—

"Millie! Come back in the room!" Lauren is calling out to me.

"Sorry," I say. "I was just thinking about Erin Breeler. Beautiful people can make you drift off, can't they? Erin and Danny. Lovely Danny with his lovely—"

"Bag!" Lauren interrupts. "Have you seen it, Millie? That boy has serious stationery."

Lauren likes paper and pens more than anything. She has a Pinterest board that is just fluorescent markers.

"I was going to say his eyes, but, anyway, Loz, I'd better go."

Lauren gives me a huge hug. She also wishes me luck, which I'm going to need.

The truth is, I could stay here for ever.

I feel sick. I don't want to go home.

#FAMILYMATTERS

When I get home, Mum still isn't back from the weekly big Saturday shop. Gary is cleaning the toaster and telling it off for hoarding little bits of bread. This is normal. He has a feud with the toaster. He says it's a bad design. The toaster feels the same way about Gary but cannot talk.

Actually, I don't think Gary is speaking to me after I damaged his robot true love. He looks up when I come in but then goes back to cleaning. Who spends their weekend doing that? Someone with no friends who likes telling things off. Worryingly, there is no sign of McWhirter.

I go upstairs to my bedroom and Dave comes and joins me. We are refugees from Gary "Neat Freak" Woolton's Democratic Republic of Clean. I create crumbs. Dave sheds hair. We are the enemy.

I keep thinking about what Mum is going to say when I tell her about Dad's. I can't decide if she'll be relieved or calm or—

She's going to be cross. Who am I kidding? I try to take my mind off things. What will my new thumbnail be? A grab of something I've watched? A photo I've taken? Mum's furious, sobbing face?

Finally, I hear her coming through the front door. I take Dave downstairs. Mum is in the kitchen, soaking, flustered and loaded with bags from Sainsbury's. A soggy French stick is poking out of one of them, and wet carbs always put her in a REALLY foul mood.

I know I should probably wait for her to take her coat off and try and have a proper sensible chat, but it's rushing up inside of me. I end up yelling at her so loudly that Dave leaps in the air. So high that if I'd been filming it, the video would have been a YouTube sensation: "Supercat scales a building".

"Mum! I want to go and live with Dad."

Mum just carries on unpacking. She must have heard, but I try again just in case.

"Mum – I want to go and live with Dad! At Grandad's house. It's a REAL place. It has a roof. It's FINE!"

This has been building up all summer, so surely it can't come as a surprise.

Mum wraps the soggy French stick in a tea towel, hands it to Gary and says, very calmly, "Of course you do, Mills. It's like the Wild West over at your Grandad's. Your Grandad tries, but you know what your dad is like. And don't get me started on Teresa. You'd be able to do what you like. You're perfectly OK here. I know you think some of my rules are over the top but turning the wireless off at night means your brain gets a rest! I'm looking after you! Protecting you! Now stop being silly and tell me what's really wrong."

This makes me cross. How could she not have noticed how unhappy Gary has been making me? I try and take a deep breath, but my brain goes on heavy-rain-flood mode, and my mouth gushes out all sorts of horror.

"Mum, eating a custard cream in this house has become a five-stage process, involving a dustpan and brush. And you DO NOT need a side plate to eat a banana! A banana is a big solid mass. It has its own neat little container – its actual skin! It's the most interior-design-friendly fruit known to man. It loves being clean. Why are we even discussing how tidy food naturally is? See what Gary's done to us?! And stop staring at my hand."

I realize I have picked up a banana and I am banging it up and down to back up every point I am making. Fruit torture is not a good look.

Mum says, "You're going to bruise that, Millie."

Gary is already brandishing a newspaper in case I make the banana fully mushy and he has to wrap it up for the bin. He can't help himself. He then starts pretending this argument is not happening and begins what he would call a "light clean" of the kitchen units.

I don't care. I am on a serious rant.

"Mum, I don't mind your timetables. Your stupid rules. Mostly, I can put up with them! BUT NO ONE CAN LIVE LIKE THIS. We used to have great times together. Now we NEVER do. You've changed. And you've always said, don't change for anyone. Don't change for a man. But that is exactly what you've done. Call yourself a feminist? You're actually a sappy, dappy cheeseball love lady. You're not my mum any more. You're HIS gooey girlfriend!" I point at Gary, who has frozen mid-polish. "And you don't let me decide stuff for myself. Like when I do my homework or how late I stay at Lauren's. Even though I never do anything wrong. I don't ever get to do anything my way. It always has to be your way and it isn't fair."

All this is terrible, but it is how I feel.

Gary "Neat Freak" Woolton, who is NOT my dad, shouts, "Go to your room!"

Mum, who is still my mum, says quietly, "What's happened to my lovely, sensible, clever girl?"

I yell, "She's in a … a coma of really fed-up!" Which is a totally rubbish response but I'm really angry.

When I storm out of the room, I trip over McWhirter, who is probably trying to escape all the noise. It completely ruins my exit, but at least he is still alive. My Aunty Teresa would call this karma. I call it further evidence of my life being ruined by cleaning equipment. Vacuum sabotage. I bet Gary programmed him that way.

#NOTADIVA

Are you still here? I'm surprised. I'm a bit horrible. I'm sorry you had to witness that.

I curl up on my bed and have a mini cry. A wrong-time-of-the-month sort of sob at a sad film. I can see Mum loves Gary. The calm part of my brain can see he makes her laugh and he rubs her dry heels with cocoa butter. She'd been single for years because she didn't want to settle for second best. Gary came along with his posh mountain bike and amazingly expensive muesli and – BANG! – it was major relationship time. So believe me, I don't want to ruin my mum's happiness.

But if I'm honest, the whole situation is making me really unhappy. This house feels like a ride at a theme park that never stops and I can't get off. And it's not making me feel good. My chest feels tight all the time. And the thing is, in that argument with Mum, I didn't even sound like me. I'm usually totally chilled and...

OK, let's just say it – sensible.

It's a CURSE. I've always been that way. I blame Mrs Woods. She wrote in my school report: *Millie is a girl with plenty of common sense.* How did she know? Well, when Stephen Pearson broke his arm skidding on the playground pretending to be an owl, I was the one who suggested we should probably call an ambulance. Everyone else was trying to find a phone to get a photo. Including, probably, Mrs Woods.

I was nine.

I know. Sweet. But also a bit tragic.

You can be anything at school. Geeky with geek chic, do cosplay or be a MAJOR member of the Nerdverse – that's basically ALL FINE. No one cares. Bradley Sanderson in Year 10 has a vlog called "The King of Elevation", where he films himself in lifts or going up and down escalators. One of his videos has 77,000 views! That's way more than Erin has ever got for one of her mindful-in-mohair posts. To some people – admittedly not many at school – HE is the BOMB.

But me? Being the sort of person that is quite … wise? Well, I'm less cool than Daniel Gyver from Year 11, who can chew through six entire biros in one Geography lesson, including the metal nibs.

My friends love me. Mum says I've got a good ear and a soft shoulder. She doesn't mean I've got a floppy, mushy body (sorry – you probably realized that). She means I usually know what to do in a crisis. Even the sort of crisis that Lauren says makes you hide in your bedroom for days eating crisps and playing *Pet Doctor*.

I can usually cope with my crazy family. I can even cope with real men. I've had a REAL BOYFRIEND. Dylan Anthony. Yes! Him! HE was mine. For a month and a half. Until we had a massive row over the suffragettes. He thought they were overreacting. I said not having a vote JUST because you're a girl was a pretty big deal.

I know. I sound like a right doofus. But in that moment, it just felt RIGHT. This is why I feel so panicky now. I'm not normally the one having a meltdown. I'm not the one who makes any silly decisions, and yet here I am about to…

It is *not* sensible to want to leave your mum and go and live with a man who still lives with his own dad at the age of thirty-eight, and once used elastic bands and a copy of *Mixmag* magazine to make you a nappy.

There is not much common sense there, Mrs Woods. But this is what I want to do.

Perhaps I just need time. Some time to stop being a wobbling mess. I'm not a dessert shaking in a desert. I'm Millie. I'm—

I need to go.

For once, I'm going to follow my heart, and my head can just … shut up, be quiet and DO ONE. If it possibly can. And if it can't, my heart can go out partying alone and my brain can stay home with a tub of ice cream and watch a film.

I must be nervous. Can't stop thinking of puddings. CLASSIC sign.

#HEARTACHE

After some mumbling downstairs, Mum comes up to see me. She's in tough mode. I can tell because her eye is twitching. This happens to both of us when we are angry. It's a genetic numpty gene we share.

"Mills," she says, sitting next to me on my bed.

Sitting next to me. You'll recognize that as a brilliant parent tactic that's meant to say, "I'm on your level. I understand."

I don't think she does.

"I understand it's difficult to share me with Gary—"

She definitely doesn't understand.

"You're not a tube of Pringles, Mum!"

"No – but you're used to having me to yourself. And now I've got someone else to focus on."

I'm quite calm now. "Someone else," I say, "who has completely insane levels of cleanliness. He tried to use an antiseptic wipe on a cushion the other day—"

"He struggles with Dave. He's never had pets," Mum interrupts.

"Whatever, Mum. Dave cleans herself at least twice a day. She would probably use deodorant if they made the can paw-friendly."

I'm still calm. Ish.

"Millie," Mum whispers, putting her arm around me. "You're right. Dave is a very clean cat. And you are a good girl. You're self-regulating." (What does this mean – she's always using it?!) "When you were a toddler, you would ask to go to bed. You've always been…"

We cuckoo together like Grandad's manky clock, "Sensible."

"I've rung your dad. He's really happy to have you. And he says you can take Dave – but, Millie, I don't want you to go! I won't stop you if that's what you REALLY want, but in that magnificent head and heart of yours, I know *you know* that THIS is a bad idea. You're back at school. You need stability. You know you do!"

How does Mum do it?! She's straight into the whole of me like a drone with a really clever missile. And she carries on. She can read me like a book that has hardly any words and lots of pictures.

"Perhaps we can work together and find a compromise to stop all this? How about the wireless goes off at 10 p.m. and we all, as a family, have a conference about crumbs?"

This makes me smile even though I don't want to. I put my head down so Mum can't see. I know she's trying to make me laugh.

"You know," Mum says softly, "Gary is a lovely guy. Yes – he's very house-proud but he also makes me laugh a lot. He's funny, Millie, and kind. Give him a chance."

I don't believe this for one minute. The Neat Freak is probably already planning to turn my bedroom into the Museum of Sanitation (that's a good word stolen from the hand dryers at school), to display his collection of SERIOUS dusters.

"Come on, Millie." Mum puts her arm round my shoulder.

"You know I just want the best for my little girl."

And THAT is the problem. To Mum, I am still that little girl in a doctor costume trying to wrap Dave's ear with a dishcloth. She won't let me actually become an adult. Moving out is really the only way to show her and Gary that I AM one. Or nearly am one.

I snuggle into her shoulder. "Mum, I love you but I really want to go and live with Dad. Just for a bit. I think some time away from here will be good for me."

Mum looks hurt but keeps her arm round me. She takes a deep breath. "OK. Well, I don't want you to go. Even for a little while," Mum says. "But you'll only be down the road. And I know, whatever I might say, that you're a big girl really. I'm not going to stop you if that's what you *really* want to do. Perhaps you'll appreciate what you have here and you'll come back with…"

She stops talking and sadly plods out of my room. I hear her sniff. Please let it be a sudden allergy to pet hair and not tears.

Oh Mum! I want to stay. I want HIM to go. IT IS HIM! I don't mind your rules, homework, even the way you tell me I shouldn't have a boyfriend till I'm thirty-two. I just want him to go and for you to let me be normal and live in the twenty-first century.

But I don't say that. I text Lauren to tell her what's happened. Then I go downstairs to tell Mum I will pack some overnight stuff and my school uniform and come back for the rest next weekend. I don't speak to Gary. *Thanks, Head, for still being a little bit my boss.*

I think.

Before I go and put my things in the car, I take a photo of my room and put it on Instagram. All my books and my lights shaped like cacti. With a Slumber filter, it looks really cool. It also means

I can check in the future to see if anyone has moved anything, or tried to scrub it. Don't mess with me, Gary. I am basically a forensic policewoman scientist thingy and I can trace your every cleaning move.

By the time I leave home, I already have a couple of likes. I'm collecting witnesses. AND they like the way I've done my room!

My old room.

What am I doing? *Brain, come back from holiday.*

I'm going to live with my dad.

#MYFAM

As Mum and I drive to Grandad's, I think about what's just happened. Mum's car is a good place to think. She drives like a granny and keeps within the speed limit even when there isn't a sign or a safety camera. I can turn off reality and overthink things.

Yes. This has been very … civilized really. That's the word to use when everyone behaves themselves and acts in a way that won't get them on daytime telly, yelling at each other. My family are like that really. We have slightly barking streaks of loon (Aunty Teresa), but mainly the team works, as Dad says. This is because:

@Parents

My parents are divorced, but in the most lovely way possible. Dad and Mum met in Ibiza when they were ravers. Mum used to wear neon bikinis and cowboy hats. But after I turned four, Mum and me came back here for school. Dad stayed in Spain and ran a club then a tapas bar then a bungee-jump business. He came back a year ago and he's still looking for something permanent, so he lives with Grandad. Mum and Dad still seem to really like each other – they just don't want to live with each other. I know! It's really unusual, but it's good for me. Dad seems to understand how difficult it is to be my age. I think Mum has forgotten. And Gary Woolton was never young at all. Bet he's never even been to a party. Except maybe to clean up afterwards.

@Grandad

Grandad is my dad's dad and is basically OK. He's a massive sexist. This is because he was born before feminism was actually invented. BUT he loves me, and sort of doesn't think of me as a girl. He always says, "You're different to most women, Millie. You don't nag, you don't cry and you don't shout at me for having muddy fingernails." This is shocking and you'll be thinking, *How do you even deal with that man?* Look – you just have to remember he's ancient, and that occasionally he gives me five pounds from his pension money to buy something nice. HA!

@Aunty Teresa

Aunty Teresa is La Diva Mentalis. She got this nickname from a Spanish man called Juan she was engaged to, until she found out he was married to someone else from Estonia. She is SO unlucky with guys *and* work, so she lives with my grandad too. Occasionally. She's also lived in a garage, in her friend's conservatory for six months and even in a tent in a field near Glastonbury. She thought if she pitched up there, went all River Cottage and lived off the land, she'd eventually get free entry to the festival. She lasted five days. And made herself ill eating poisonous berries. I've basically looked after her since I was born, even though she is twenty-seven years older than me. At a job interview once, they asked her if she had any questions and she said, "What's the best way to get rid of verrucas?" You see – I have to be sensible, as a lot of the so-called adults around me are not…

@Dave

Dave the cat is actually a girl. Don't ask. I was three. My mum asked me what I'd like to call her and I said Dave. It's the most stupid thing I've done, but it sort of suits her. She's a feline rebel who lives on the edge. Actually, she's mainly just asleep and trying to pinch your crisps but she's my cat and we understand each other.

So things were working OK until Gary came along. I lived with Mum and we would go to Grandad's every week for Sunday lunch and after school on a Friday. But now I'm going to Grandad's for much more than that. I just need to look on the positive side of all of this: no more iron rules, no more set bedtimes, no more homework times, no more being followed around with a dustpan and brush and a can of furniture polish.

Oh, why do I feel so … nervous? I keep getting this feeling in my tummy like a knot. A big lump of worry.

Dave is not happy inside the cat basket. She looks very grumpy. Cages don't fit with her rebel credentials. I tickle her chin through the bars. She's pushed all her grey tabby fur through the wire and does a massive tuna breath hiss at me. I have to be strong. For Dave. She's going to miss the hedge where she waits for wild-bird burgers.

Come on, Millie. Pull it together.

That's me talking to me by the way. Dave can't talk. Yet.

#GLOWSTICKDAD

When we get to Grandad's, Dad is GLOWING. I've made his Saturday night – and probably his life – complete. He gives me a huge hug and says, "MILLS! You've come to live with lads that love you. We are going to have so much FUN! I've made your bedroom up. Pop upstairs and put your stuff down."

Mum stands at the front door looking sad. The outside security light makes her look like a Doctor Who villain. She is not. She is lovely. I see her mouth at Dad, "Look after her."

Dad mouths back, "Of course I will."

I say goodbye to Mum and she says something, but no one can hear anything as Dave is howling to be let out. It sounds like she is in pain but she isn't. She's having a major tantrum. By the time I've stuck my finger in to rub her head (she bites it), Mum has gone.

Luckily, Grandad arrives with a hot piece of chicken and gives Dave a gourmet snack with one of his super crinkly old fingers. Dave goes to purr factor ten and shuts up. Grandad also gives me a piece and whispers, "Roast meat makes everything on earth happy."

I think the chicken would disagree but now is not the time to go militant vegetarian. Grandad hugs me and I go upstairs with Dave.

Dad has done quite a good job on my new room. He has moved his bongo drums and taken out most of Aunty Teresa's junk. There's still her collection of cuddly toys and Sylvanian Families though. If you move those things, she'll go into full panic mode and have to breathe into a bag. I've seen it.

So there are miniature rabbits and a massive Winnie the Pooh, but I notice there's no actual clothes rail. "Dad – where can I put my school uniform and stuff?"

"Well, I thought you could hang it over Aunty Teresa's exercise bike. She got it on eBay and was going to use it for half an hour during *Hollyoaks* but she never got round to it. It's not for ever – just till we … till we … get you something … more appropriate. Anyway, settle yourself in, Lady Mills. I'll go and finish tea. Will the usual Dad special be OK?"

I tell him it will be fine.

It isn't really but he looks so happy I don't really want to make a fuss or make him feel bad.

I put my jeans over the exercise bike, take a photo, Instagram it and write:

Sometimes you have to make the best of what you have. Meet my wardrobe… #fail

Dad won't mind. He understands the banter. No one will see it anyway. I'm not Erin Breeler. I haven't got worldwide followers hanging on my every word.

What I have got is chips and mayonnaise with a salad cream coulis waiting for me. Not #glam but #myfam.

#LIKEAVALANCHE

When I check my phone after my gooey tea, I get a bit of a shock. The first thing I see is a message from Lauren.

`Mills. Massive post! What's your Dad's like? x`

It's unbelievable that, in under an hour, a stupid thing about a piece of abandoned bike that was bought in a panic from an eBay New Year's sale has had some shares and LOADS of likes! Plus, I've got thirty-two new followers. And it's quite late and the Wi-Fi is still on! Coming here was the right decision! This is all the savoury stuffing balls of amazing.

Just as I'm scrolling through all the comments (**My mum uses her mini trampoline as a shoe rack!**), Lauren calls me.

"Have you seen? Have you seen?!" she is screeching down the phone.

"Yeah," I say. "It was only a stupid thing about my dad's place. It's not—"

"But Millie — you're funny loads of the time, and you notice things that other people don't. Look how often you make things better by making me smile. You NEVER fail. And Gracie messaged me. Her sister is in Year 11 and was talking about you! Apparently, loads of them are dying at the panda thing that you did to cheer me up. They've shared it everywhere! Have a look! You're just GOOD. Honestly, I think you should do a proper vlog or something! Not Instagram 'cos that's Erin, but a vlog!"

"Come on, Lauren. I'm not that interesting. I'm not like −" (and this is the first person who leaps into my mind) − "the Mad Baltic Boy Scientist and his dangerous slime baths."

"But you could be! Sort of. I mean, you're not a boy and I think you shouldn't do vlogs involving paddling pools and explosives. But, seriously, I know other people would totally love you. You could do it from your bedroom. You could start off by talking about how to deal with insane aunties and their exercise bikes... Just try it! YOLO!"

YOLO. You only live once. It's Lauren's favourite phrase. She uses it whenever she wants me to do something a bit brave or out of the ordinary. I'm not always so good at doing this. Because ... all right, I will tell you. But PLEASE don't think I'm being boring...

#YOLOSBC

I'm going to be dead honest with you. I'm a bit of a worrier. I get very anxious. It's why I'm on the more … what does Mum call it? The cautious side.

I think it might have started when Mum got run over when I was six. She broke her pelvis and was in hospital for ages. I don't remember a lot of it but I do remember seeing her in plaster up to her actual face and thinking, *Oh don't leave me, Mum.* It just seems like the world is a really dangerous place. And when you google stuff, it gets worse. 650,000 car accidents a year are caused by random insects. A plane once crashed because of some wasps in a tiny tube. There's a jellyfish the size of a fingernail that can kill you! OK, it's very unlikely to be in Devon, where we normally go on holiday, but still! Stepladders, scarfs, lawnmowers, cows! All these things have caused serious injuries, you know.

I'd better not google accidents caused by exercise bikes. That'll be another thing to worry about.

Grandad gets it. He seems to see through me. He says Grandma was like it. The Swan, he called her. She looked graceful on the outside but underneath, where no one could see, she was paddling like mad. Mum gets it too. Or used to, before Gary.

So, YES, Lauren. You only live once. So be careful.

This is why I like my bedroom so much. You've got your friends on Messenger and you've got people on YouTube who just want to make you laugh or help you put your lippy and blusher on the right way. AND you've got people that seem quite happy to jump into frozen lakes dressed as lizards to promote their band. You can watch other people do the risky stuff. I CAN STAY SAFE.

Who am I kidding? Your bedroom is also the place where trolls can say what they like about you. Or where you can see the photos Mr Style Shame has posted of you looking like a massive spoon.

Perhaps Lauren is right. Perhaps I should start #YOLOing and just GO FOR IT. I've broken free from Mum and the Neat Freak. Perhaps I am braver than I thought? Better than I thought? And being a panda to cheer up Lauren was pretty epic. Perhaps I should just do a vlog? Instagram is great, but with a vlog you can TALK to people. Have a laugh. Perhaps I should just put the camera on now and just … just…

What?

What sort of stuff should I talk about? I can't talk about fashion or beauty – and anyway hundreds of vloggers are already doing it way better than me. Could I pretend to be an animal other than a panda? Maybe my speciality is just comedy bears.

Dave is looking at me. Right now, I think she'd make a better vlogger than me and she's currently trying to attack my cardigan and eat her own tail at the same time.

#GRUMPYCAT

When I wake up, I realize the following:

1. I've had the worst night's sleep ever mainly because I kept checking my phone every five minutes. I now have 1,086 likes on my bike photo and 859 views of the panda vlog. This is what it must feel like to be Erin Breeler. It's good. I like it.

2. I am wearing Aunty Teresa's Christmas pudding beanie as this is actually a fridge pretending to be a house.

3. Dave is staring at me from the end of the bed.

4. Lauren is also staring at me from the end of the bed.

"Who let you in?" I love my friends but I don't expect them to be actually in the duvet with me on a Sunday morning.

"Er … no one," Lauren whispers. "I just let myself in."

I should have remembered. This is not Mum's house with its super-sensitive burglar alarm and multiple locks. This is Grandad's house. There might as well be a massive human cat flap where the front door is.

Lauren is giving me her full-on serious face. She looks like an aye-aye monkey. Cute but slightly terrifying.

"Mills. This is… This is… Right … this is…"

"This is what, Loz?"

Lauren's cheeks twitch because her face is allergic to being sensible. If eyebrows could do Pilates… I'm expecting something a bit life-changing because she looks like she's about to burst.

"This is a bit epic, Mills. TITANIC."

And then she makes a massive movement with her hands like something has exploded in a microwave and covered the kitchen in baked beans. And no – not even I cover mine with cling film. Like Dad says, life is too short to give food an overcoat.

All this makes me giggle.

My laughing makes Lauren cross. "Seriously though, Millie. LOOK at your exercise bike pic. Someone has even said, **This is everything. Give me more of your life hacks** and LOOK who has liked that comment!"

I scroll through them again. Danny Trudeau thinks it's a good idea. The new boy has noticed me.

This is not a massive deal. How many random things do you like in a day? Bet you can't name them. I can't. Plus, I'm not about impressing men. I do silly stuff for me.

Lauren won't be stopped. "You could be a major Internet star. I've been thinking about it ALL night. You should do … something. I just can't think of what."

Dave jumps into Lauren's lap and lies on her back with her paws straight in the air. She truly does not care about anything or anyone. She does what she likes when she—

It's then that it hits me. I grab hold of Dave. "CATS!"

Lauren starts shouting, "Yes! Let's make Dave a vlogging superstar! Cats always get likes."

"I'm not sure Dave will though, Lozza. I don't think she understands vlogging. But let's have a go anyway?"

I get my phone out, look straight into the camera and start recording.

"This is Dave and I'm Millie. You see a lot of entertaining cats online. But Dave isn't like the cats you usually see on here."

At this point, Lauren catches on and pulls out a packet of Doritos from her bag. She tries to balance a Dorito on Dave's nose. Dave just lies there with her legs still in the air. Lauren then piles up a cuddly llama (Aunty Teresa's), a science textbook (mine) and a chicken Marengo sandwich (Lauren's – it looks vile) around Dave.

Dave still just lies there on her back. I carry on.

"As you can see, if you want to make your cat go viral, get a cat that at least reacts to bread."

At that moment, Aunty Teresa bursts into my bedroom with her masses of black curly hair and her very neon spotty shirt. She's like a big cloud of slightly manic. She's also really loud. She takes one look at Lauren and Dave and shouts, "I'm sorry to barge in, Mills, but I heard what you've been talking about and all I'm saying is, VEGETABLES!"

I pause recording. I don't want to look completely stupid. Suddenly, you can see what I've been saying about Aunty Teresa makes quite a lot of sense.

Lauren looks puzzled for about half a second, then her and Aunty Teresa start jumping in the air yelling, "VEGETABLES! VEGETABLES!!!"

I sit there spoonlike.

"Haven't you seen it?!" Lauren is looking at me like I've suddenly grown four extra heads and an arm.

The worry rises in me like a tight anxiety burp. Usually "Haven't you seen it?!" means something involving you that everyone else knows about and you don't. I whisper, "Seen what?"

"MILLIE! Where have you been?!" Lauren says, getting her phone out. She shows me a cat jumping ten metres in the air after being ambushed by a cucumber. Apparently this is a thing – this cat has had over five million views and four figure likes.

A cucumber. Probably the most un-terrifying vegetable except for turnips and they are pathetic AND unpopular.

Aunty Teresa dashes downstairs and brings back a real-life cucumber, three potatoes, a mandarin and a cauliflower. We remove the sandwich from Dave and for the next twenty minutes, we film Dave with vegetables.

This includes:

- Lauren putting a cucumber by Dave. Dave cuddles it.
- Aunty Teresa rolling potatoes in front of Dave. Dave ignores them.
- Lauren giving Dave fake eyebrows with mandarin segments. This is quite funny.
- Lauren making Dave a small helmet for Dave from cauliflower leaves. Dave pulls them off in a really undramatic way.

Then I get a message that the storage is nearly full on my phone.

"There you are! How NOT to make a cat vlog with me, Millie Porter, Lauren and Aunty Teresa!"

As I press stop, MUM thunders into the bedroom like a really cross elephant in gym kit, and Dave decides to rear up on two legs, leap two metres in the air, do a somersault and land perfectly. The camera is OFF.

Lauren is very impressed. "Wow, Mrs Porter, can you just do that again so I can turn the camera on and … get…"

You can tell by my mum's face that it really is time to totally shut up. Aunty Teresa has a rare moment of being a bit sensitive and grabs hold of Lauren. "Anyway, do you want to go and increase our brain bandwidth with some more vlog ideas?"

Lauren says, "Er … yeah," and they disappear really quickly. It's just me, Mum and Dave.

"Millie," Mum says, "I've brought some more of your stuff round. I thought you might want your school things sooner rather than later. And why have you got a piece of holly on your head?"

"I'm a Christmas pudding – it's cold," I snap. It's very difficult to be taken seriously when you are a dessert or a panda.

Mum shakes her head and leaves. She shouts, "I'm going to unload the car." I hear her muttering as she trips over something on the stairs. That would never happen at her house.

I should be using this time to go and help her, but I'm not. I'm going to keep my stupid hat on and edit and upload my new vlog. I think the bit with the cucumber was actually quite good. Family can wait a bit. It's vlog o'clock.

#GIRLPOWER

Now I have to admit by the time Mum has carried all my stuff up to my room, I'm feeling a bit cross. I've only been here for one night and Mum is already checking up on me.

I bet I know why she's here. Mum reckoned I'd be ready to come home after one night. I used to hate sleepovers when I was little. So Mum thought I'd get panicky almost immediately and go back to hers before she knew it. Her plan has failed! I am stronger than she thinks!

I can tell that she is worried though. She keeps walking around my new room picking things up and putting them down again, as she opens and closes her mouth without a word. She looks like a music video on mute.

She tries to be nice. "Millie. If you are going to live here, you are going to have to make some little changes. They are ones that you deserve! The front door needs a proper lock. You need somewhere to hang your clothes. And a desk for homework. And someone needs to remove THAT garden gnome that's doing you know what from the porch."

I know which one she means but I say, "I've not noticed it. What

I have noticed is how I can walk round this house without being attacked by a mop!"

"Well," Mum continues, "that's partly why I'm here. After you left last night, I had a chat with Gary. He has agreed to get McWhir— the robot vacuum cleaner out ONLY every other day. So I want you to know that HE is prepared to meet you halfway on the issue that maybe, *perhaps*, he is over-cleaning."

"I'm not meeting anyone halfway!" I shout. Mum has ALWAYS told me that a strong woman doesn't give in. She fights for more. So I say, "Mum. I would like to see a complete cess–cess—"

Mum interrupts me and helps me with the word *cessation*.

"Yes," I continue in frankly a very-professional-almost-bossing-the-entire-situation way. "A complete cessation of the robot-hoover issue."

Mum looks sadly at me. "Well, Millie. That's not going to happen. Nor should it. Gary is trying. I'm trying. So should you. That's what ADULTS do."

The old Millie would have just shut up and done as she was told. But this is not old Millie. This is NEW Millie. Independent Millie. RESURGENT Millie (I stole that from a film). RESURGENT MILLIE AHOY! And THIS Millie can fight back.

"Well, MUM. I AM in a house full of adults and THEY actually act like grown-ups rather than super controlling crazed people!"

At that moment, we both hear Dad shout from the kitchen, "Teresa! We cannot start using paper plates just because you don't want to spoil your Halloween nails by doing the washing-up. I don't care how long it took to do the Vampire bat. Anyway, it's SEPTEMBER! It's TOO EARLY. Even for YOU!"

Mum only has to look at me and say, "You'll always have a room at my house, Millie. Come home."

And then she flounces out in a dazzle of Lycra. My mum rocks gym kit. She rocks everything.

She is totally magnificent and everything I would like to be. I can't tell her that though. I'm too upset.

Downstairs, things have escalated. Teresa is claiming you can scrub the bath by just having a bath when you are already clean and "rolling about a bit".

Wherever I live, cleaning causes problems.

I put some TV on and doze. It's all been a bit much. Too much emotional stuff sends me sleepy. Especially if I'm wearing a duvet.

When I wake up, I check my phone and squeal loud enough to make a dog deaf.

#FAVOURITE

My cat vlog has already had over a thousand views, which must be because it has been liked by the DAILY DANESH and he has COMMENTED!

Great cat. Chilled. Funny. Purrfect Pet, YEAAHHHH. All the thumbs.

The Daily Danesh is one of the BEST vloggers around. The boy who lives with his gran and created the game of Fridge-Freezer Jenga (he made a 151 cm tower of fishfingers and potato wedges!). He's a LEGEND and he HAS SEEN ME. He must like the fact that my female cat is called Dave.

It seems Dave not being a viral sensation is actually quite funny. I can see in other places that the vlog's been shared by loads of people at school … including Danny Trudeau.

I think he's just trying to sort of be "in" with everyone.

You can stop thinking that. No. He does not fancy me. He doesn't even know me! This is real life, not Disney. Boys like him don't fall into big hug time with girls like me. You know what I mean.

I take a screengrab and change my bio to **Favourited by the**

Daily Danesh as this is huge and just what I needed after my mum made me feel like I was about seven years old.

I run downstairs to tell everyone. Teresa and Dad are having a foot fight. So I tell Grandad instead. He's not very impressed. In fact, he's rude.

"So someone you have never met before and have absolutely no idea what is REALLY like decides that you have said something a bit good and pressed some sort of thumb symbol thing and that's a cause for celebration?!"

I leap in the air, clap and shout, "YES!"

"I know you're a clever girl, Millie," Grandad mumbles, "but I'm not going to get excited every time something tiny like that happens. You'll get a big head and there's nothing worse than that. Especially in a woman."

I don't really want to do that "old people don't get it" thing but OLD PEOPLE REALLY DON'T GET IT, do they? Plus, perhaps if Grandad had given more praise to his children, they wouldn't currently be practising WWF wrestling on the front-room carpet – they're in their thirties!

Also, "Especially in a woman?!" I decide to make it my responsibility while I'm here to drag Grandad into this century with some epic feminism.

Slightly deflated, I go back upstairs to the room that is not really my room. I realize that I didn't even say goodbye to my actual best friend due to my family's non-stop drama. I message her.

Sorry for earlier Loz. Will think about vlogs that aren't about Mrs Mad Cat! See you tomoz. BTW Daily Danesh liked it!

I don't want to show off, but I am chuffed and minted and all the joys.

Lauren replies almost immediately with 200 emojis and:

`Class Mills. C-L-A-S-S!`

It's an OK response but, between you and me, I'm a bit disappointed. This is my best friend and the Daily Danesh is big, so I reply:

`Are you OK?`

If I'm being really honest with you, that really means, "That was a bit of a rubbish message. Why? Are you OK?"

My phone pings, like, IMMEDIATELY.

`No. They are yelling again. It's horrible.`

INSTANT GUILT. Why am I getting excited about a like when Lauren basically lives in the equivalent of one of those really horrible places you see on television where there's constant war?

I message back.

`Stay out of it. Do what I do when it gets too much. Put your headphones on, do some colouring and remember, I think you ARE THE BEST.`

Lauren sends back loads of hearts. Send the love. Feel the love. It's what you have to do, isn't it? That is just properly sensible.

Can I tell you what I've noticed? That not many adults are feeling the love. Lauren's parents argue pretty much 24/7 about everything. During the summer holidays, while me and Lauren watched *Harry Potter and the Deathly Hallows,* her mum and dad had a row about everything from Lauren's swimming lessons (she didn't want to go) to Lauren's gerbil (was it dead or just really tired?) that lasted the ENTIRE film. When a boy wizard can save the entire world in the same time that you have screamed about a dead mouse thing, you should probably realize you have problems.

My problem is that I can't stop checking the views on my vlog. Maybe now Danny has seen me online, I can actually say hi to him in real life at school tomorrow?

Or maybe I'll just stay quiet and safe and UNDER THE RADAR in real life.

#PARENTPLAN

When I see Lauren at school the next day before registration, she looks tired. "They shouted till about 2 a.m.," she moans. She pulls the books out of her locker in the corridor like she hates everything. "Millie. It was pretty horrible. It was slightly funny though when I heard my dad say, 'The way you arrange the spice rack is madness!' It's very difficult dealing with people who get really angry about coriander and ground nutmeg."

Lauren smiles but looks like she's about to sob too. It's times like this when your best friend needs a lift, so I change the subject.

"What about the next vlog?" I'm talking very quietly because I don't want anyone else to know just yet. "How about a How NOT To Be a Parent vlog? You and me have got lots of personal experience we could share."

Lauren does a little jump in the air. She brightens up pretty much immediately. "I LOVE IT, MILLS! The point is it's a global, universal issue. Like gaming. And make-up. All the big vlogs are about the stuff that is worldwide and really matters. Like cats and really amazing cakes."

I decide to just come out with it. "We could talk about your parents!"

Now I know this is touchy, so I quickly say, "But we could disguise ourselves."

Lauren stares at me intensely. "We could totally wear huge wigs."

"Hm. Maybe not." I don't tell her that's possibly the worst idea in the world. I just gently say, "But I think if we start off by talking about it from our own—"

Lauren interrupts, "Like if I talk about the argument last night. I mean loads of parents probably argue about swimming, gerbils and the precise placement of herbs in the spice rack."

I can sense she is being sarcastic.

"Actually, they probably do, Lauren. I bet that argument has happened the world over. I bet that if we did a vlog about that, we'd—"

Suddenly, the atmosphere around us goes icy cold. A shadow appears. We've been spotted. Hunted. Cornered.

"Well, well, well! Look who it is! Millie Porter! We ARE causing a bit of a stir, aren't we?"

Abandon the plans. Put all defences up. Erin Breeler is coming this way.

#COPYCAT

Erin Breeler is not what you need first thing on a Monday morning. She is officially the worst start to the week since I had tonsillitis at Christmas.

She glides up to both of us like she is on demon fairy wheels. Miranda, her fluffy best friend, is by her side. Erin towers over us and we press our backs against our lockers. She is tanned and made up brilliantly. Her lashes flutter like a flock of butterflies. Do butterflies come in flocks? They do on Erin's eyes. Seriously, if I didn't hate her so much, I'd be completely impressed. I try and keep calm but inside, I feel the fear. My palms are sweating and leaving big print marks on my Maths book.

She purrs at us. And it's not a Dave-style purr. "All praise the Wardrobe Queen!" she laughs. "What a clever use of a piece of exercise equipment. I'm impressed, Millie. Really."

"Er … yeah," I say. This is RUBBISH. Why can't I think of something better? It's like that time Dad wrapped Aunty Teresa's head in Sellotape. She couldn't say or do a thing. JUST LIKE ME NOW.

"I really did think it was good," Erin continues. "An unexpectedly funny, smart post."

I've still got mental tape all around my brain and body so I just say, "Thank you."

"It was so good," Erin carries on, "I thought it could do with a little bit of … improvement."

Suddenly, something in my head springs back into action.

"And what form would that 'improvement' take, Erin?" I sound a bit tough but not too ridiculous.

"It's no big deal, Millie. It's just about knowing what you're doing on Instagram. I mean, what you did was great, but you can't hope for too big a reach without … upping your game."

Now my tummy isn't fully of Erin's butterflies. It's full of buffaloes – galloping through fields, trampling everything in their path. My stomach is just a mass of HOOVES.

"And how would I do that?" I just about manage to get that out despite the total body stampede.

Erin smirks her perfect smirk. She pulls out her phone, tosses it slightly in the air and catches it perfectly. It's Cirque du Soleil with the latest Samsung. "Using good filters. Posting at the right time. Decent hashtags. The right audience for the content. That sort of thing. But it's OK, Millie, because I like to help if I can."

Feeling ever so slightly like I'm going to throw up, I ask her what she's done.

"Oh, don't let me tell you, Millie. Have a look. Look and … LEARN. Oh, and Lauren, I thought those heels were fab. It's just a shame how some people can't cope with real fashion but I'm sure you'll get there eventually!" Then she flounces off down the corridor with Miranda, who just smirks and nods like a smirky, noddy thing.

I grab hold of my phone and go straight to Erin's account. When I see what she's done, I want to go off like Gary when he's spotted pink mould in the shower.

Erin "TOTAL EVIL" Breeler has reposted my photo onto her account, given it a different, and, YES, much better filter and got hundreds of likes in under an hour. What is even worse, she has captioned it:

Don't fancy getting fit? Don't worry, girls, here's a great hack from @MilliePorter. If you're not a #GymBunny, you can always use your kit as your wardrobe instead. Remember if you want to make high-street fashion last, take care of your clothes ;) #glow #Primarni #LifeHacks

Erin looks back and sees that I have seen her evil. "It's a great message, Millie," she shouts. "I like helping people. You're helping them too, Millie. We did it together. It's like…" And she pauses and does that face of MAXIMUM MINX. "It's like me and you, for that tiny minute, were a team."

Then she walks off. She's a trap and I just stepped right in her.

We can't speak. We don't say anything for about three hours. It might be less than that but it feels that long. Lauren just stares at me and finally says, "How does she manage to always be … right?"

I sigh. "She's clever. This is a whole new world of terrible, Lauren. Even when you do good stuff, she finds a way to make you feel terrible about it. Now all her followers will think I'm a complete spoon and troll me to death."

"What do you think we should do?" At times like this, Lauren assumes I have the answer, and usually I do. But not this time.

"Well, there's nothing that we can do – we've just got to take it and…"

"And?" Lauren puts her arm round me.

"I need to think," I say.

Actually, I need to think for a very long time.

#ZENLOO

At lunchtime, I find my quiet secret place. I need it sometimes. No. I can't tell you. It's secret.

OK. Furthest cubicle to the right nearest the Science Block. Trust me, it's Zen Central.

Most people have no idea what power words have these days. Mum told me once that a group of girls used to stand at the end of her street and call her names. There were six of them. She told me that story like she was majorly traumatized. Six people in one street in one town. That's IT! That's all.

How to explain to her that now there can be thousands and millions of people laughing at you within a minute of you doing something stupid. Or NOT even that stupid. The sort of people that follow Erin are going to be laughing at me, thinking I'm tragic.

I take some deep breaths. Sometimes it's best not to think about things too much.

I don't fire back and do something rash because that's not my style. You've got to plan, and I'm a thinker.

First, I'm going to think about my breathing. Normally, my lungs work just fine by themselves but now I start noticing that my chest is going up and down. My body seems to get smaller. It happens every time I'm really worried. And I can keep it together by just being on my own for a few minutes. Nipping off to the Zen loo is always a very good idea.

I come out. Lauren has been waiting for me outside. She's used to this. She doesn't say anything but she knows.

I'm calm.

Or I am until I spot Danny Trudeau and his incredible vintage orange rucksack. They are heading my way like a sexy tangerine and my BFF is frantically digging me in the ribs. Happening now – panic.

"Hi, Millie!" Danny bounds over to me like we are old friends. We aren't. I wish we were. "I just want to say I absolutely loved your vlog with Dave the cat. Someone mentioned it in Art this morning and I was… It was FUNNY. I'm a cat freak though. I love them. I had to leave mine behind in Canada with my uncle. His name is Benny. I Skype him but cats aren't great at the talking thing. A bit like the way Dave isn't that great at attacking vegetables. Anyway, your vlog was … really good."

I don't really know what to say. I'm not hugely good at the whole compliment thing. But I don't want to be giggly and stupid near men, so I try and change the subject. I jog around my head trying to think of something funny and witty and magnificent to say. Something that will make this boy think I'm cool and smart and generally…

"You've got a great-looking lunch there!"

You've. Got. A. Great. Looking. Lunch. There.

But no, my brain hasn't stopped. It wants to say more.

"Good container too. Sturdy!"

Dear Sensible Millie's Mind. Thanks for nothing. Goodbye.

Danny Trudeau looks at me like I've said something really random. This is because I have said something really random. Eventually, he replies with "Yeah! Chinese mum. French dad. The world's best food all in one box."

"A la noodles!" my head blurts out. If Danny thought I was funny before, my brain has convinced him that I am actually not.

Danny smiles a bit and looks down. There's a pause and then he says, "Well ... I'd better be going to ... finish this. Bye, Millie. Hello – is it Lauren? You were in that vlog too! Bye, Lauren!"

Lauren manages to wave. My brain hasn't recovered from the "A la noodles!" comment and can't form a sentence.

Danny Trudeau and his gourmet lunch drift off like steam. I collapse on a bench. Lauren drops beside me with her jaw on the floor.

"What happened there?!" Lauren isn't used to seeing me so utterly useless. "You were... Oh Millie! You really like him, don't you?!"

I groan.

Lauren puts her arm round me. "Don't worry! Perhaps he likes talking about ... kitchen storage."

In the middle of saying it, Lauren realizes she sounds ridiculous and tries something else. "He thinks you're really funny!"

I have a bad feeling that Danny Trudeau and lots of other people are laughing AT me not WITH me. I really need to get away from school as soon as I can.

#DADRESCUE

When I get home, I find that Dad has taken all the cuddly toys from my bedroom and the exercise bike is now in the hall. Apparently, Mum gave him strict orders to make a lovely room for me. Yes! But I feel a bit bad. The bike is now a place to put coats, junk mail, charity collection bags and the red bills that my dad seems to get all the time. It will never be something to increase your actual fitness on.

Grandad corners me when I go downstairs to make a cup of tea.

"You look fed up, love. Everything OK?"

I tell him nearly everything. I can see him looking puzzled. Finally, he blurts out, "I don't get it. Why are you bothered by the opinions of people you've never met in your life, orchestrated by some madam who needs taking down a peg or two? Just ignore her!"

But I can tell that he's worried because I hear him go straight into the front room and tell Dad that I'm being that "new style of modernly bullied".

Dad come upstairs, hugs me and says, "Mills, do you want me to go up to the school and sort this out?"

I show him the photo. "Here's the problem. I posted the photo.

I shared it first. She's just shared it again, credited me like she should have done, but basically said I'm tragic. She's done nothing wrong. Really. Well, she has but she's – Dad, she is EXTREMELY clever. You can't beat her."

Dad stares at me intensely and says, "You're right, Millie. Keep away from her. She's clearly a bit of a genius. Focus on your friends. You're still friends with Lauren, aren't you?"

That isn't really what I wanted to hear. I wanted more than that. God, I miss Mum. She'd know what to do.

Dad goes back downstairs and, despite my frankly enormous clever bit of brain YELLING, "Don't read the comments, Millie!", I can't help myself. I look at Erin's account again. The likes have gone up to over 1,000 and the comments are *horrible*:

Who would live like that? Selfish to the earth

Awful jeans! No point taking care of those LOL

SLOTH! :-)

Great advice E

Wow, that room could do with a decent tidy and a paint job.

Now I know I've been moaning a bit about my room, but Dad is trying and Grandad is old! He doesn't care about repainting.

This person needs to get some self-respect for themselves and their clothes.

Just as I can feel my chest getting tight again, I see another comment:

Erin – you are just evil for doing this. Stop being so fake.

It's from @MissLaurenMeister – Lauren's account. She's brave and loyal and lovely … and very, very stupid.

#PARASOL

I call Lauren immediately. Every second that comment is on there, someone could see it and report back. And when Erin sees the notification or hears about it, she isn't going to be happy that someone has accused her of being less than perfect in front of her followers. She will take things even more nuclear. Use Weapons of Mass Social Media Destruction.

Lauren picks up the phone after no rings. "I know, I know," she yelps, "but I just can't take that girl any longer. We have to stand up to her, Millie. We have to stick our heads above the parasol!"

"Parapet," I have to correct her.

"Yeah, whatever – what is a parapet?"

I google it. "It's a barrier which is an extension of a wall at the edge of a roof."

"Yes!" Lauren shouts. "We need to stick our entire bodies over the social-media parapet and put up an anti-Erin parasol to guard against her onslaught of being … fantastic. I'll delete the comment though. Hopefully, she's waxing and hasn't seen it!"

I tell Lauren my plan. I've been thinking about it since the corridor clash this morning. "I reckon the best way to fight back is to make another vlog that makes US number one at school. And then no one will remember Mr Style Shame or the exercise bike."

"YES! But we've got to do it RIGHT. The right name. The right look. The right EVERYTHING. We HAVE to take it as seriously as Erin. She basically has a brand."

"You're right, Lauren. No more cats or pandas or How NOT To vlogs. This is going to be the real thing. You do realize though," I say, "that this means she will go for us, Loz? It's not just sticking our head above the parasol."

"Parapet! Now you're getting it wrong!" Lauren giggles.

This makes me laugh too. "Yes. That. Again. This is sticking our head above the entire world and saying, 'ERIN BREELER! We are here with our vlog and it's about the things that REALLY matter. It's the stuff-that-really-matters vlog!' I know! How about we talk about how we deal with school, home, boys, make-up – we can cover everything?! EVERYTHING THAT MATTERS EVER AND EVERYTHING THAT WILL EVER MATTER! And we can start with…"

I tail off. I sound ridiculous.

"Yeah. This might need a bit of thought, Mills." Lauren sounds uncomfortable. "And what should we call it? If we're taking on Erin, we can't sound like spoons."

She's right.

Lauren pauses and whispers, "Perhaps we can make up a really smart pseudo cyber bully called Helen Teeler?!"

"Oh Lozza, I'm not sure that will work. I know – I'll come over after school tomorrow and we can discuss and plan fully."

I get off the phone and trip over a tennis ball that has rolled out from under the bed. Our next vlog will have to be filmed somewhere quiet where there is little chance of someone barking coming in and, when I hear Teresa singing about her latest Tinder date, I know that means not here.

#ONLOCATION

"Well, we can't film it here, Mills. Listen!"

When we get back to Lauren's house, her parents are not shouting. It's silent. And immaculately tidy. Perfect conditions for vlogging in fact.

"Why can't we?" I ask.

"Because it's always really quiet before they kick off again."

This annoys me a bit. I was counting on Lauren's house. I know her parents are rubbish but I'm not in a great domestic situation either! Surely we can make a vlog without them getting in the way. I try to persuade her.

"But we can't do it at my grandad's. It's chaos and no one understands privacy. Aunty Teresa comes into my bedroom every other minute."

Lauren bows her head. "Millie. We can't do it here."

"Are you sure?" The vlog is such a good idea I don't want to let it go AND I want to get it just right.

"Millie. There's a football match on tonight. Mum wants to watch it. Dad doesn't. That makes Dad rant about old girlfriends and the way Mum still wears floral dresses and Doc Martens even though she's forty-one."

This outrages me! "But they look cool though! That's totally sexist!"

"I know," Lauren sighs. "He's just cross. He doesn't really mean it."

This makes me think. "We should do a vlog on discrimination too, Loz. There are loads of things to cover. Feminism. Sexism. Should you wear make-up when you're campaigning for a better, fairer world? Or something."

"Whatever, Millie, we can't do it here. Seriously."

I have another major breaking-news brain flash of excellence. "I know where we can do it. We'll have to time it just right though. My mum's house. I don't want to go back there but ... my room would be perfect!"

Lauren looks horrified. "But you're not living there any more!"

"I know!" I wink. "But I've still got my key."

"What about the Neat Freak?" Lauren asks.

"He works late on Wednesdays and Thursdays. If we time it right with his shifts and Mum's, we'll be fine! Tomorrow after school. We'll have exactly forty-five minutes. We can DO THIS! TRUST ME!"

This is me pulling out my credit card of sensible. It never lets me down.

#BURGLARS

We go straight from school to my mum's. It's deathly quiet. We creep up to my old bedroom and open the door. It's Wednesday and the Gary's away. The normal world can play!

When I get inside, I can see that someone has already dusted the blinds, even to the far corner bits. No one does that. I bet even Prince Harry's blinds are filthy bad there. It looks cleaner than it has done in a very long time. And it was only a bit dirty in the first place. I am fully aware of all the many diseases that come from dust and bed mites. I've seen those photos of bedbugs that have been magnified to a million times their actual size.

"Right," Lauren says. "First things first. What's our vlog going to be about?"

I flip out some notes I've scribbled down. Mum always says preparation stops poor performance. WHY can't I get Mum out of my head?

"EPIC!" Lauren shouts. "Now we need to prepare THE FACES."

Lauren's make-up collection is extensive. Her mum and dad buy her something every time they feel guilty about shouting and upsetting her. Which is a lot.

We spend serious time getting the base right, and then we thoroughly contour for screen. We go high gloss on the lips and dark on the eyes.

Lauren looks at us both. "Yes. The effect is professional but approachable. It says we mean business but you can also talk to us on a level that you're comfortable with. It's the look of today's pressurized professional woman. We work. We nurture. We deliver."

I try not to laugh but I do. "Loz, you spoon, where did you get that from?"

Lauren laughs too. "I saw it on *This Morning* when I was off school with conjunctivitis. Seriously. It's make-up with a message."

We both end up giggling like mad. "Loz, we need to be quiet. If Mum finds out we were here, she'll think that I can't cope at Grandad's."

"Well, you can't." Lauren looks all sheepish and apologetic. "You're Miss Lady of Order and that house feels like a party popper has just gone off ALL THE TIME."

I do a death stare. "No. It's not right for vlogging. That's different."

Lauren can see I'm a bit miffed so she just takes some fairy lights off my mirror and dangles them in the air above my head.

"Shall I hold the lights like this behind you?"

I do not want my best friend standing behind me like a Christmas tree. It will make us look like those wacky funster vloggers. That's not what we're about. I'm not saying we can't be funny but we also have really serious stuff to discuss.

"Loz, I want you sitting with me. OK – how should we start? I've been thinking our first subject should be—"

Lauren interrupts me. "Well, I thought we could just say who we are … and then totally wing it. Be natural. Talk from the heart!" And then she just stares at me.

I try not to get cross. I do think we need to be a little more prepared than that. But I don't want to be too bossy and Mrs Know-It-All to Lauren. That's old Millie. Mum-influenced Millie. I'm trying to live more in the moment now, so I say, "Yeah! Let's go for it."

I press record on my phone and we both say, "Hello!" then collapse into giggles.

"It's OK! We can edit it!" I say. "Take two. Take two."

"Take two what?!" Lauren looks very confused.

"That's what directors say," I explain. "TAKE two! OK. This one. Really this one."

We turn the camera on and giggle again.

"Lauren!" I yell.

"I'm sorry," she snorts through laughs. "It's just, you know … too … you know!"

"I know." I get it. "Right. Let's think of something really serious."

Lauren stares at me and says, "Death."

And we still can't stop laughing.

"What is wrong with us?!" I ask. "Are we terrible people?! We're now laughing at death!"

And then Lauren collapses on my fluffy rug, shaking with the giggles.

"It's not even funny," I yell but I can't stop laughing either.

Then suddenly, I hear a noise outside the door. "Lauren. Shhhhh! I think Mum's back! Or Gary!"

Someone is coming down the landing towards my bedroom.

We've been making so much noise, they must think we're really rubbish burglars. My heart starts to pound. I can see Lauren looking at me for comfort but I can't give her any. I'm scared too.

She whispers, "What if they bash us over the head with something or call the police? Or call the police THEN bash us over the head?!"

"Shhhh!" I snap. "It's going to be OK." I don't believe this for one moment.

The door creaks open slightly. Someone is checking to see who the intruders are. Unless… My brain starts an insane worry spiral. What if burglars are actually disturbing US? What if some prisoners have escaped and they want a really tidy safe house with a good selection of soups and non-crumbly biscuits. We are in trouble. I can sense it. I know it. This is bad. This is serious.

This is—

McWhirter, the robot vacuum cleaner, glides into the room on full spin and starts trying to hoover up Lauren, who is still on the floor. He must be pre-programmed to start cleaning automatically. He has a little base on the landing that he sits in when he's doing the upstairs.

I scream very angrily, "McWhirter!"

"Don't upset him." Lauren looks nervous. "Perhaps he'll tell Gary or something!"

"How can he, Lauren?! He's a robot!"

Lauren narrows her eyes. "Perhaps he has a surveillance device on him. Perhaps a tiny camera is relaying all this to your mum now via satellite. Perhaps she doesn't really work at a hospital. Perhaps she's been employed by the government to spy on teenagers everywhere and robot vacuums are actually just cameras that clean!"

It's then that I decide we need to get out of here.

"Lauren. We are catching crazy off this house. This is why I wanted to go to Grandad's in the first place. Let's get out of here."

"What about the vlog?" Lauren looks GUTTED. This is her big dream too.

"We just need another plan. We're not giving up. Let's go back to mine, get some dinner and have a think." I put my arm round her.

I haven't got a clue where we could film, but Lauren doesn't need to know that right now.

#SHEDOFSENSE

When we get back to Grandad's, Dad and Teresa are having a karaoke session. Teresa is in the middle of a serious power ballad. Dad is howling like a dog in pain. They have loads of fun together but no one has done the important jobs. A duvet of lint has collected in the back of the tumble dryer. The house is Mess HQ and it's why everything is on the brink of catching fire.

The safest thing is to go out to see Grandad. As usual, he's in his shed. He spends a lot of time there. He may not understand women or the Internet, but perhaps he has some idea of a place to film that is slightly sane and quiet.

I knock on the shed door. Lauren waits outside. The shed can fit two but not three. Grandad is sitting there asking a tiny rose in a tiny pot why "she" refuses to bud. Though this sounds a bit mad, it's easier to deal with than what's happening indoors.

"Grandad, can you…?"

All of a sudden, I have an odd thought.

Grandad's shed would be a perfect vlogging space if we just moved all the gardening equipment, the pot plants, the green netting, his tools and pieces of wood, and his calendar featuring

Britain's favourite seashore wading birds.

Grandad spots me eyeing it up. "I imagine you want to come in here for some reason. Quiet. Nice big inside lock that keeps the whole world out. I may let you use this shed, but don't you be taking my bar-tailed godwit, Millie. I want that calendar kept up there."

Grandad is slightly psychic.

"I was just wondering if me and Lauren could use your shed for a bit of filming. We want to make a vlog," I say.

Grandad looks at me with his detective-inspector-investigating-a-murder face. "What's a vlog? Is it illegal?"

"No, Grandad! It's like a video that you can upload to a site and then everyone can watch it!"

"But why would people want to watch it?"

Grandad doesn't mean to be harsh. He just really does not get it.

"Because," I explain, "you've got something to tell people that might help them or make them laugh or—"

"So what are you going to tell them? What can YOU do?"

OK. He IS sounding harsh now. And Captain Sexist of HMS *Patronizing*.

When I answer him, I sound a bit sharp. "I'm starting a funny advice vlog. On how to deal with life and idiots and families and trolls."

Grandad stares at me. "You do know trolls aren't real, don't you, Millie? I mean, I know we told you they lived under bridges and frightened the Billy Goats Gruff but they—"

I do lose my patience slightly now. "Grandad. A troll is someone who keeps hassling you on social media and the Internet." I try to make it simple. Lauren nods behind me.

"Well, just tell them to stop it," Grandad says.

I'm trying to be patient. I REALLY am. "It doesn't work like that. You can tell them to stop it and they just carry on."

Grandad looks angry and his fists clench. He shouts, "Tell a teacher then. Or me. I could sort them out for you, love."

This melts me a bit, but I don't know where to start.

"The thing is, you don't always know who they are, Grandad." I'm thinking of Mr Style Shame. "Or you can't prove they are really being horrible." Now I'm thinking of Erin Breeler.

Grandad looks at me. "Millie. I don't know if I want you being in that world much."

"That world? It *is* the world," I yell.

"Well, young ladies have to look after themselves."

Grandad has a thing about young ladies having to be careful. It makes me cross.

"So do young gentlemen," I snap. "Please can I use this shed?"

"You can use it, Millie. Because you're not a daft girl. Your dad's crackers gene missed you. But … just be careful. Look after yourself then look after everyone else."

Grandad always says this to me. It seems a bit selfish to me but he is selfish. He had all his washing done and dinner made for him for thirty-five years. He doesn't really understand thinking about others.

But he's helping me, so I just give him a hug and say, "Thank you."

Grandad nods. As he goes out of the shed, he says, "By the way, I'll sort the tumble dryer before the whole place goes up."

Grandad is like me. He likes me. He gets me. I love him.

I call Lauren in. "Grandad says we can use his shed for the vlog!"

Lauren says, "You sure, Mills? It's not very glam."

I explain that we don't have an alternative and we are NOT allowed to touch the bird calendar.

Lauren looks disgusted. "We can't do a serious vlog with a bird in the background."

I can see her point. "Let's change it to a different month," I suggest. "Perhaps there will be a better bird."

Lauren flips through the common sandpiper, the curlew and the whimbrel before she asks me whether the Temminck's stint looks "a bit sexy with its incredible Olympic cyclist legs".

I give her a bit of a look. "It's a bird!" My best friend's gone off the planet. I need to get her back. "Leave it on the bar-tailed godwit," I tell her. "Let's get started. Grandad's not going to let us stay in here for ever."

Lauren pulls her super serious face. There's a long pause before she murmurs, "You know, I honestly think you should do it on your own."

"What?!" The whole point was that this is something good that Lauren and me can do TOGETHER.

"Look, Mills, all I'll end up doing is repeating what you say AND interrupting you! I'll sound STUPID. I didn't even want to do it that much at your mum's. Seriously. I thought I would want to but I don't."

"Lauren, I'm gutted. Please do it with me!" I'm begging a bit now but I don't care. "You're funny and people love you. You don't even have to try! And you look amazing!"

Lauren's eyes are on the floor.

"No. You do it on your own, but I want to direct, do your make-up, dress the set and perhaps be off camera."

And then Lauren admits the real reason why she doesn't want to be on-screen. "I just hate how I look even WITH the contouring. I looked like such a spoon on Mr Style Shame. I hate my legs. And when I speak on camera, I get twenty-five chins!"

This makes me really angry. "Everyone has twenty-five chins, Lauren! If you didn't have all those, your neck would split and your head would fall off."

Perhaps we should vlog about that. People who don't want to be on film because they hate the way they look, even when they are totally wrong about that.

"I don't want to talk about it, Mills," Lauren snaps.

I get it.

"Have you been trolled? Lauren! Don't look! Turn them off!"

This is great advice but I don't know if I would follow it.

Lauren gets angry. "Millie. I don't want to talk about it but I can help with the other things. If I'm going to direct and dress the set, I'm going to tell you what I really think. Before you do your first vlog, you could do with some expert advice so it looks good. I don't mean YOU looking good. I mean IT looking good. We're in a shed. We need all the help we can get. Who do we know that does great videos or stuff online?"

"Erin Breeler and loads of famous people who won't help us." Yes. I'm getting breathless again now. This was exciting. Now it's going bad very quickly.

"We do know someone who can help," Lauren says, sort of sheepishly. "Bradley Sanderson."

"Bradley Sanderson? The king of lifts and escalators?! But we're not going to be vlogging about machines."

"It doesn't matter what he vlogs about, Millie. The point is, he does it really well. He gets loads of views! You should ask him about it at school tomorrow. And keep out of Erin's way."

Erin. She'd make my advice vlog into something about birdwatching and wading birds in an instant. I can't imagine her EVER posting anything filmed in a potting shed. Lauren is totally right. I need James Bond's geek genius, the one who sorts out his gadgets. I need Bradley Sanderson to be my secret weapon.

#GEEKHELP

It is not as simple to find Bradley Sanderson as I thought. I try on Thursday lunchtime. We are not meant to use our phones in school hours, so I suspect he is hiding in the shadows somewhere. It can't be easy to have a hugely successful but absolutely terminally dorky vlog. Your friends must be mainly online not offline.

I try the library, the computer lab, the empty Year 10 classrooms and just about every corner that exists in school. Eventually, I lift up a massive furry parka on the coat racks. Bradley is hidden underneath. With just the light of his phone in his eyes, he looks really spooky. He has thick-rimmed geek-chic glasses and a floppy fringe. His hair is like a blind he can pull across his face.

"What do you want?" Bradley looks up at me.

"Hello, Bradley. I'm Millie Porter from Year 8. I was wondering if you could help me with my vlog?" I'm feeling a bit nervous about talking to him.

"Ah! A damsel in distress. 'Help me, Obi-Wan!' she says. 'You're my only hope.' I don't think we've met before, but yet now, because it's vlogging, you want my help!"

I think Bradley is being a bit snarky. Maybe I'm not the

first person to try and make friends with him for socia media advice. I'm clearly out of my depth but I want to learn. So I carry on.

"Well, you're a bit like a famous bat. We all know about you, but no one sees you in daylight. You have loads of subscribers, Bradley. Please can you let me know your secret?"

This seems to soften Bradley a bit. "What's your vlog about?"

I sit beside him underneath a blazer. It feels weird but right at the same time. I try to explain. "Well, I want to make a vlog that will help people. People who don't always fit in at school or are finding it hard at home or who are being trolled. But it's not going to be all Captain Dullard advice. It will be silly too!"

Bradley looks down at his phone. I get the sense that this might not be the greatest idea for a vlog he's ever heard. "Vlogs are easy. Do it in landscape on your phone. Download an app. The app talks to your laptop. Upload and edit."

Bradley clearly thinks I am very stupid indeed. Talk about mansplaining.

"I know all that. I mean, how do you get people really interested? How do you get people to subscribe? What's the right way to talk to your subscribers?"

Bradley looks up again and smiles. "Millie. I'm happy to give you advice. But it isn't as simple as having the right hashtags or uploading stuff regularly."

"But Bradley, I really, really need some help! I've never done this before. All I've got is my grandad's shed and a best friend who's great at contouring! And a cat!"

I'm feeling pretty desperate and it's starting to get rather hot under this blazer. "Look, I'm not being funny, but can we come out from under these blazers and I'll—"

Suddenly, the coats lift up and I see something that takes every single bit of oxygen away from my body, even though that isn't actually possible or I would die.

Looking at both of us is Danny Trudeau.

I lose control of some of my atoms and my brain blurts out the first thing it can think of. "We are not kissing!" I bark, pointing at Bradley.

Bradley agrees so quickly it's almost a bit rude. "No. We are NOT."

"Hello, Millie! And don't worry, it's none of my business." Danny beams. His smile is like the Northern Lights. Probably. It's certainly like that really beautiful screen saver featuring the sky at night with all the stars. "It's just that's my blazer." He gestures to the coat I've currently got draped over my sweating forehead.

As I try and untangle myself, going EVEN redder in the process, I manage to blurt out some words. "We're just talking about vlogging!"

Danny leans on a locker and winks. "Of course you were. Sorry to disturb you!"

I don't want him to go. So I keep talking. "Yeah, so I'm thinking of doing an advice vlog. Sort of following on from the other stuff I've done with the bike, the panda and Dave."

This sounds ridiculous when I say it out loud.

"Who's Dave?" asks Bradley.

Danny purses his lips together. "Yeah... That sounds..." When he thinks, he gets a crease in his forehead. "Yeah!" Suddenly, he brightens. "I know! You could call it something short and quick and memorable, like … #Help!"

I leap up. "#Help! Danny, that's actually fantastic. Thank you!"

"It was your idea." Danny says. "I was just your muse."

I have no idea what he means, so I just say, "Yes!"

"Anyway!" Danny exclaims. "I've got to go. Enjoy your brainstorm." Then he drifts off like he's being carried by wings. And not the wings of a wading bird. The wings of a mighty hot eagle.

When I regain a sort of sensible consciousness, Bradley is giving me a funny look. It's almost like he feels sorry for me. "Now THAT conversation, Millie Porter from Year 8, would have made a great vlog!"

I regain some dignity. A bit.

"I was just a bit shocked at … that, but I need your help. I don't want to beg. I've got a name for it now at least! Will you please help me do something actually, possibly useful?"

Bradley sighs. "Come to the shopping centre on Saturday. They've had Schindler MRL traction scenic elevators installed. Believe me, they are world class. I've had requests to film them."

"You've had people asking to see them?!" I find this very surprising.

"Yes, Millie. My vlog has got global reach. Meet me there on Saturday at 2 p.m. I'll try and help you a bit."

"It's a date!" I quickly correct myself. "Well, it's not a date but you know what I mean. It's a date."

"Don't worry, Millie. I've got a girlfriend. She likes lifts too. This isn't a date."

"I never knew you had a girlfriend! What year is she in?" This is turning into a day of quite enormous surprises.

Bradley puffs up his chest and says in a rather cocky way, "She lives in the States. She's mainly into walking pavements and scenic escalators. That's how we met. Online. I want to fly over to see her next year but my mum doesn't really get it."

"They never get it. My mum is lovely but she'd freak out if she knew I was thinking about vlogging."

Bradley raises one eyebrow. "She'll find out, Millie. They always do. If you have any success, she'll find out. See you Saturday. Got to go. Double Maths. Some relief from the hell that is this place." Bradley disappears, sort of clinging to the wall in a way that makes him invisible to other people.

Really, I should get to class. Really, I should tell Mum what I'm doing. Really, I should do a lot of things, but I'm too busy thinking about the fact Danny last saw me when I was pretending to be a pile of coats.

I am turning into a boy idiot. I need to stop. I hate it when girls go like that. Dumping their friends for men and being ridiculous. And besides, we all know what is going to happen to Danny Trudeau.

#PREDICTABLE

"He is totally going to end up going out with Erin Breeler."

During the Thursday afternoon torture that is Shakespeare, Lauren manages to say what the whole of our year is thinking. And it's a real tragedy.

"I know," I whisper. "I spoke to him at lunch and thought exactly the same thing. He even SMELLS good. Like a really expensive oil diffuser."

Lauren giggles. "Expensive oil diffuser?! Like Gary has in his car? Christmas Spruce and Gingerbread? But how have you been close enough to him to smell him?"

How to explain this one? "I was under the coats with Bradley Sanderson and he disturbed us."

Lauren looks like she has developed seriously miffed disease and hisses, "I think your next vlog should be about when you don't tell your best friend actually the biggest things that are happening in your life right now."

I have to spend the next five minutes reassuring Lauren that we were just having an undercover vlogging masterclass. Which was her idea in the first place. When I finally convince her that she'll be the first to know WHENEVER I kiss someone, she shouts, "Now TELL ME what you found out about Danny!"

The class goes quiet. Erin Breeler and Miranda turn around and look at us. Once we have been told to calm down by Mrs Foss and are safely holding our copies of *Romeo and Juliet* in front of our faces, I have to admit that I don't know a lot more than she does. But I do tell her that he had the idea for #Help.

Lauren grunts. "There's a photo of him on Instagram. Well, of his back. Have you seen it?"

We hide my phone in my pencil case and find the photo. It's on Leanne Pilton's Instagram, which is mainly full of her dog. She managed to basically pap the back of the lovely. He looks Big Ben tall and has a fantastic bum even in regulation school trousers.

"Should we be looking at a photo of a bum?" I ask Lauren. "I feel a bit wrong and sweaty. As feminists, we have a go at boys who do that to girls."

We stop looking. It's hard but as Mum says, principles are often hard to carry but that doesn't mean you should drop them. I keep the image in the guilty bit of my mind though.

I know Lauren is still thinking about it too. She starts off discussing the latest Mr Style Shame post, but midway through talking about what everyone is now calling "the Pug Print disaster", she changes the subject.

"You should share that you've spoken to him and that you like him, Millie. You're basically being a journalist by doing that. It's the breaking news everyone wants to know. OR you could just comment on Leanne's photo and say something like, 'Canada's a great place and full of quite excellent people' and then just add loads of winky faces and hearts. We'll know what you mean!"

The truth is, I do like him. Even more after the coat incident. It's not just his looks. It's his whole vibe. And why shouldn't I tell people I met him and he was nice?! I'm going to do just as Lauren says. That's what a strong woman does. I can't worry about what other people think ALL the time. I can't worry what Erin might do, or even if Danny sees it. That's sensible. I am sensible. IT IS SENSIBLE TO LIKE CANADA and share that fact. I have decided.

#TWOFACED

When I check my phone between lessons, I find that the Canadian High Commission in London and someone called Annabelle D'Sa have hearted my post. I suppose it doesn't really matter that actually the entire country of Canada thinks I love it.

Lauren agrees. "They are probably nice people too. Their flag has a leaf on it that looks really approachable and friendly."

How can a leaf look friendly?

Lauren googles it. "Look at it! It's sort of jumping in the air and saying, 'Come in … to my hot tree!'"

"You're off your tree, Lauren – that's the basic problem."

We collapse into giggles.

"Seriously though, Mills, we mustn't get distracted from the vlog. Let's see how things are going on the Dave one. Maybe someone's got an idea for #Help." Lauren flicks the phone out from her pocket.

The numbers haven't changed from last time. Not one more like. Not one more view.

I'm a bit gutted by this. However much #Help means to us, it's probably not going to be a success. How do people even become popular?! How do you win against all the celebrities, people jumping into frozen swimming pools and experiments involving gunge and massive water balloons?! Or the Erin Breelers of this world?

Lauren sees I'm down. "You know what you've got to do. When you see Bradley Sanderson on Saturday, you HAVE to get him to tell you how he gets so many hits for his stuff about boring stairs. Then we can start vlogging properly."

I will, but after today, I'm not sure he's going to tell me that much. I think he's probably just being kind. He's only really interested in his own thing though. Between you and me, I admire him.

Anyway, I should just get over myself and ask for more advice.

"Yeah. You should … ask … or talk or … whatever you think is the right thing, Mills." Lauren seems distracted. "Sorry!" She looks embarrassed. "I'm looking at the Instagram photo of the Canadian bottom again."

I'm still a bit uncomfortable with it. I would hate it if someone did that to me, but I just have a quick look. It is fabulous. It's a really tremendous view of someone's back. Since I commented on it, it's got loads of likes and more comments, including—

"Lauren. LOOK at the comments!" We're late for History now, but I am FULL of rage. We read it together.

I hope @LeanneP asked permission from @DannyTruds before posting this #creepy

It's from Erin.

She's also replied to my comment about Canada with the embarrassed monkey emoji. Maybe my Danny love wasn't so subtle after all.

Lauren points to the phone and says every word in slow motion.

"Can you EVEN believe the total hypocritical, two-facedness of it! After what she did to you with the exercise bike. She really is a major piece of work."

I know the real reason why Erin is going Miss Social Media Moral. Hot boys unofficially belong to her till she says otherwise. And she has to be the first to know all the gossip. Still, we've been warned… I explain this to Lauren and she looks really impressed.

"You are basically a psychologist, Millie," she says. "You just need to do a vlog that's actually good and doesn't make you sound like a seven-year-old spoon that has just got hold of his mum's phone while she's hanging out the washing."

I death-stare Lauren.

"It's a compliment. Sort of," she says.

#FAKEFEMINISM

I am not wise. I'm certainly not brave. If I like Danny, I shouldn't let Erin stop me from trying to get to know him. I should be asking for his number, not writing messages about Canada.

And that's pathetic, isn't it? I am completely changing what I do, just so she ignores me. That's not wise. It's dumb.

I think about all this during History and miss some key points about World War One. This makes me feel completely guilty because clearly it was totally dreadful and really mattered.

The end-of-school beeper charges me out of a total spiral of worry. Lauren rushes over to me brandishing her phone with a face of total fury. "LOOK! HOW. DOES. SHE. DO. IT?!"

I look. There for all to see and already with thirty-two likes is a selfie of Erin and Danny. It's a fantastic aerial shot. She's obviously used her extender stick and the mobile cover she has with back lighting. The filter makes them both look even better-looking than normal.

Erin has captioned the picture:

Welcome to @DannyTruds from Ontario #NewBoy. Thank you, Danny, for letting me post this cute selfie! And let me tell you

all, my new BBF (Best Boy Friend, before you ask) is a keeper ;)
Remember girls, #StrongMen like #StrongWomen and don't be
too shy to make a boy your friend #Feminism

"Can you even believe it?" Lauren says. "The truth is, no
one has been more evil to you or to me than Erin Breeler. If
being a feminist means you are nice to all women, then she is
not one."

I don't think feminism means that. It means we as females
believe we are entitled to be treated equally and ought to have
the same opportunities as men. And that we should not be judged
completely on how we look.

Lauren has a different point of view. "Well I think it should be
about being nice to women. And if it's about not being judged JUST
on how we look, then I am not taking anything from a woman who
has an Instagram account about how fabulous she looks!"

Lauren does have a point there, but Erin has SLAIN us on this
one. She bags Mr Beautiful Boy AND gets to sound like a cool and
independent woman who doesn't look at secret photos of men's
bums and is great at life advice.

"One good thing!" Lauren shouts excitedly. "It's completely
fine to stare at his photo now. Danny Trudeau. He sounds like an
amazing range of car tyre that would never let you down in any sort
of terrain! He's way out of our league, Millie."

Lauren is right, but this makes me cross. "Why is he? We are
good-looking, funny, clever women of today. He'd be lucky to go
out with either of us."

I don't believe this but as Aunty Teresa says, fake it till you can
make it.

"Yes, Millie." Lauren rolls her eyes. "There is no doubt in my mind you're going to end up married to him."

This is Erin's fault. She makes Lauren sarcastic and me either frightened or ridiculous.

Lauren doesn't need to say it. We all know who he'll end up going out with. Erin might be pretending that she's got a new guy friend, but we know her game. No way is she letting him out of her sight now. She will share the picture of their first official coffee, the first time at the cinema and the first lovely photo of them under a really nice tree with lots of dramatic branches. That's real life. That's how it works. We will get to see their entire annoying love affair all in the Valencia or Hefe filters. And of course I'm going to look. I know I shouldn't but I will.

And yes, MASSIVE jealousy face. Jealousy and annoyance at horrible girls snogging lovely boys IS common sense and right and would probably be approved by the Prime Minister.

#RUMBLED

When I get home from school, both Mum and Gary are waiting for me in the front room. I give MUM a hug. She looks at me with one of her eyebrows firmly planted on the ceiling and says, "Hello, Millie. Next time you come round, can you make sure I'm there? It would be lovely to actually speak to you."

I'm rumbled. "How did you know I was there?"

"Gary sensed a disturbance." Mum looks very annoyed and Gary looks very distressed. "He felt there was something slightly out of place. And you accidentally locked the robot vacuum in your room when you left and closed the door behind you. It was going berserk. Like a trapped dog. Gary was very concerned."

Gary looks at me very seriously and says, "His little motor was a bit scorched but he had a little rest and everything is OK."

I think I am meant to be relieved at this. The truth is, McWhirter is one of the few things in the world I am not worried about.

Betrayed by McWhirter. Lauren wasn't paranoid. She was right. That hoover has totally got it in for us. Mum carries on. She sounds hurt too.

"Why did you come round when we were both out? Come on,

Millie! I know you. I know it wouldn't have been for something stupid but … have things got so bad that you can't see me? What did you want to hide from me?"

What do I say? It was for something Mum would never understand and she wouldn't even want to try. She'd go crazy if I told her about the vlog.

I say, "Oh, I'd just forgotten my … onesie. It's really cold here, Mum. They don't really—"

"I know!" Mum interrupts. "You can come home, you know. Your dad's a good man but he lives in a way that's very different from what you're used to. You make good choices, Millie. And choices are what LIFE is all about. You need to make thoughtful and considered ch—"

Mum is disturbed mid-sentence by the sound of a mad car hooting. We rush to the front door, and pulling into the drive is a very battered and old ice-cream van. Teresa leans her head out of the driver's window and starts shouting, "I am Mrs Whippy! Hear me ROAR."

"It's the greatest idea ever!" Teresa yells. "I just need to get the fridges fixed, the motor tweaked a bit and the thing that plays the tune installed but I don't really need that – I can just shout, 'ICE CREAM!' out of the window. I mean, at the moment it can only go at about five miles per hour, but you don't need to go that fast when you're an ice cream van anyway, do you? I'm sure people won't mind waiting behind me. Everyone loves ice cream. Also, it's the greatest way ever to meet guys!"

At this point, Teresa finally spots my mum and Gary. "Oh, hello! How are you? Fancy sponsoring me? Seriously, this is a cast-iron business opportunity. This is a family business that can be passed down the generations!"

Mum doesn't reply to Teresa. She just looks at me and says sternly, "Choices. Decisions, Millie."

Mum can always find things to prove her point. They land in her lap. Even bad old ice-cream vans.

"Anyway," Mum continues. "Look. You're welcome at the house any time and Millie – you can tell me anything. You know that. That's how we work, me and you. Honesty. You make the right decisions normally. Please try to keep on doing that."

Gary starts violently sneezing and says, "Can we go? This place is terrible for my allergies. And yes, Rachel, I've had a squirt of my nasal spray but even that can't perform miracles."

Mum gives Teresa a hug and says, "When you get it going properly, give me a call." She knows she never will but Mum isn't nasty. She's ace. Really annoyingly ace and sensible – just living with a man who knows I was cruel to his hoover. He will never forgive me and will probably report me to the Royal Society for the Prevention of Cruelty to Vacuum Cleaners.

Mum then gives me one of those hugs that I never want to end. But it does end and she goes back to my house. Her house. Gary's house. Probably just McWhirter's house. It doesn't matter. It makes me feel … like I want to put a duvet over my head and eat biscuits.

I leave Teresa and Dad downstairs planning their gourmet ice-cream van business and lie on my bed. Erin now has over 500 likes for her photo. It is perfect. Danny is perfect. The comments say stuff like:

Gorgeous!

Your attitude is so inspiring ☺

A true #feminist #warrior

I mean, WHAT?! These people don't really know Erin. They see her photos and think she's beautiful inside and out but she's…

The fact is, I am jealous. And actually, there is a lot to learn from Erin. She takes what she does online really seriously. She plans it and filters it and takes every photo a hundred times and writes things that people love. Things that she KNOWS people will love. I can't do that because I haven't got her arch brain of evil genius, but I can take what I need to do seriously.

That's what I need to do.

I message Lauren.

`Lauren. When we do this vlog we are doing it RIGHT.`

She messages me back with:

`Learn from Bradley, Mills. He's a genius with it all.`

She is right. The Emperor of Escalators is the key to my success.

#BUTTERFLIES

Saturday morning comes around and I'm feeling really nervous. The weird thing is, it's like a date sort of nervous. When I went out with Dylan Anthony, I used to feel like this. I was worried about snogging wrong and garlic breath. But none of that matters with Bradley. He's a sweet guy but I don't "like him" like him. And as for Danny. No chance. Need to tell my head…

Dear Brain – just because there is now no chance of you going out with Danny, it does not mean that there will be tongues with Bradley Sanderson. It's just going to be stairs and vlogging advice. Get over yourself. He's got a girlfriend. Stop getting in a tizz. Stop creating a spiral of total doom and—

"Where are you going and why are you talking to yourself?" Grandad stops me by the front door. His fingernails are full of mud.

"I'm meeting my new friend Bradley." I tell him the truth. I don't want to though, as I know where it will lead.

"Oh!" Grandad is teasing me now. He winks and does a tiny jump. Actually, it's more of a raise of his heels. That's all he can manage. "A young man? Is this your boyfriend?"

Why do you always have to go through this with members of your family whenever you mention a male?

"He's JUST a friend!"

"Of course he is!" Grandad does his annoying wry smile.

"You realize you can actually be friends with a boy, Grandad? Just friends. You don't have to marry them. You can just meet them and chat!"

Grandad harrumphs. The problem is, I do sound a bit lame. A boy is teaching me how to do stuff. I'm not particularly happy about this and I'm certainly not letting Grandad know that. He still believes men are the best natural teachers. He tells his own doctor what's wrong with him before she can explain. And he calls her "nurse", even though she's a doctor.

But he's letting me live in his house and use his shed so I just smile and leave. This is not fighting for equality but it IS sensible.

That word again. Sorry. I can't help it.

ARGH! Why am I so nervous?

#LOVELIFTS

When I eventually find Bradley Sanderson in the shopping mall, he is standing inside a lift with his phone pointed at the control panel. It's lunchtime on a Saturday. The place is busy. A mum is trying to wheel her pushchair in at the same time but Bradley doesn't notice her. It's like he's totally in a world of his own.

He eventually sees me waiting outside and says, "The first thing you need for successful vlogging, Millie, is focus. Focus. Ignore everyone else around you. They are irrelevant to your key mission."

"That's all very well," says the lady with the pushchair, "but Oliver and I need to get to the florist's on the first floor."

Bradley scowls at her, presses a button and whips out through the doors just before they close.

"People who use these lifts don't understand the beauty of them. The thought that has gone into all the engineering. They just use them to go up or down. It makes me cross. Anyway, YOU. I've been thinking about your vlog. Shall we go and have a coffee?"

This is really sweet. Bradley has been thinking about me and wants to talk to me properly. I get the feeling that he doesn't think about people in general very much. I feel a bit ... honoured.

"Planning, Millie Porter!" Bradley continues once we've got a chai latte (me) and a green tea (Bradley). I insist on paying. It's the twenty-first century and this is NOT a date. "You want to bring something to your audience that they need to hear or haven't heard before. Something different. Don't assume that you are the only one that feels something. I used to be embarrassed about liking lifts but then I found out that all over the world there are lift lovers like me. And if it's not hurting anyone, then it's FINE. What advice exactly do YOU want to give?"

"I want to help people. I want to put this boring brain of mine to good use for a change, but not be boring with it. But. Yeah. I do. I want to help people who feel … BAD. I've been finding it a bit hard with my mum's new boyfriend and my best friend is having all sorts of trouble with her parents."

I feel stupid saying all this, especially to a nerdy boy in Year 10, but it's true.

Bradley seems to speak more softly. It's like he's starting to care … a bit.

"Well, you need to THINK about what you are going to say then. You have to find a way to be different. To stand out."

"What about how it looks?" I ask.

Bradley stares down his glasses. "Shock! Horror!" he says. "That doesn't matter as much as you think."

"It does to girls." I feel dreadful saying this but I have a terrible feeling that it might be true.

"I don't know about girls. Not many women are into lifts."

"Don't be sexist, Bradley." I snap at him a bit.

"It's not sexist, Millie. It's an actual fact. And anyway, you just said girls are basically only interested in how things look! That's definitely sexist."

There's a bit of a pause. I fiddle with my sugar wrapper.

Then Bradley rather casually says, "I actually think #Help is an OK idea. I'm not too keen on the name. It's a bit … North American. But I reckon you could find an audience. If you keep it down to earth. To be honest, there are times when I would watch a vlog like that."

I'm surprised Bradley is admitting this. "I didn't ever think you would need something like that." This is rather a massive lie. Sometimes massive lies are good.

Bradley knows I'm just being nice. "It's not easy being me. I might have thousands of subscribers and my own channel, but it can't have escaped your notice, Millie, that I don't really fit in at school."

I don't know what to say here. It's very true and I can't pretend it's not.

An "Um. Well…" is all I can manage.

"It's like my vlogs. I edit out all the people calling me 'weirdo' and 'geek' and 'lift lover' and the bits when I get pushed out the way."

Bradley looks really sad at this point. I start to feel a bit bad for the number of times Lauren and me have laughed at him.

I don't really know what to say, but Bradley saves me by talking about my vlog again.

"Your vlog could be useful. It would be good to be able to ask someone who is a real person AND who is the same sort of age a question and not get a massive lecture about what I should and shouldn't do. Anonymously, naturally. I don't want to be talked about. Or talked about in the bad way." He's smiling at me as he says this.

The bad way, of course, is people saying you aren't a hottie or that you're weird or a freak. If I'm being really straight with you, I doubt anyone talks much about Bradley at all, and if they do, I doubt it's in a good way. Which is bad really, because when you spend time with him, you realize he's actually … sort of kind, I suppose. I'm dreading asking the next question but I know I have to.

"Did you see the cat vlog me and Lauren did?"

"Yeah." Bradley scrunches his face up.

"Thoughts?"

"It was fun," Bradley says. His face is still scrunched up.

"And…?" I ask.

"Ok, Millie. I'm going to be straight with you." He unscrunches his face a tiny bit. "It was fun … and that's it. It was a laugh. But everybody is sort of over that, Millie. Cats were big about three years ago. And anyway, that kind of content isn't real life. It's like a perfect edited piece of it. Cats are just dull most of the time, but if you believed what you saw online, you would think everyone had a perfect ugly trampolining pet. Did you know some really popular vloggers and Instagrammers are quitting because it's got too fake? You can start living your life to fit the vlog. Everything becomes about online. And really good life and lifts can pass you by. I ignored a paternoster once because I didn't think people on the vlog would be interested. I regret it now."

I don't know what a paternoster is but I get his point and it's a bit of a revelation. I hadn't really thought about it in quite that way before.

"You know what, Bradley," I say. "I AM going to be real. I'm going to have fun but be real. Talk about real stuff. Talk about what it's REALLY like. Tell the TRUTH and look REAL and … natural. I'm not going to wear lots of make-up either. There's only one thing though. If I go completely natural and real, I will be trolled into a coma."

Bradley laughs softly. "Millie. You'll get trolled anyway. I can't pretend you won't. Just do it. People will always find fault with you. Do you think it's easy loving lifts? It's not. I'm a lift-loving cosplayer. We are basically a very-easy-to-laugh-at minority group. But who cares? Now, I've got to go and see if I can get some footage of the inner workings. It's been … really … quite OK speaking to you. Just go and do it. Yeah, just … be you."

And with that, Bradley quickly gets up and dashes up the stairs that are there for people who are terrified of lifts.

I stand there feeling like I've been with one of the wisest, sweetest, weirdest people on the planet. He shouldn't live under coats. He should spread all that brain everywhere and not just on escalators. Also, he said very lovely things about me, which makes me feel … odd.

I need to get back to Lauren before I forget all the good advice he's given me. I think we're ready to start #Help.

#DICTATORHAIR

I get the bus from the mall to Lauren's house. The whole time, I'm thinking about Bradley.

When Lauren lets me in, she looks really confused. "I'm reading something someone has shared. They want hair like a young Joseph Stalin but they don't want to show a photo of Stalin to the hairdresser."

I am very used to Lauren being a bit "out there" but this is seriously random even for her.

"And…?" I ask.

Lauren stares at me. "What's so wrong with Stalin?"

Where to start? I spend the next five minutes explaining that Stalin killed everyone who didn't agree with him, that millions starved when he was in control and that generally, he was completely horrible with a really bad moustache.

Lauren listens to all this and then holds up her phone and shows me a photo. "But, to be fair, he was really fit when he was younger. Look! He could be in a boy band."

There is absolutely no doubt that Stalin was quite attractive when he was younger, but it all comes back to what Bradley says.

How much do we let people get away with stuff in real life because they are fit and take a good photo? I'm feeling quite – what word does Mum use? – MILITANT about this.

Lauren interrupts my thoughts. "Anyway. What did the escalator geekathon spoonfest say?"

"Don't call him that!" My reaction takes me by surprise. I feel a bit protective about Bradley now.

Lauren looks at me. "Millie. I would be amazed if Bradley Sanderson didn't seriously fancy you! I mean, how many NON-dates do you think he goes on?"

"Lauren!" I snap. "It was NOT a date and he does NOT fancy me. We're just friends. He has a girlfriend. He can help me and we can both … have a good time."

Lauren drops her phone and shrieks, "YOU fancy Bradley Sanderson!"

"No!" And I really don't. "But he knows his stuff, Lozza. He says planning is the key. And he thinks that the vlog should be REALLY honest and talk about stuff that properly affects people. And –" I sort of say this really quickly – "I shouldn't wear too much make-up."

Lauren looks like I've gone mad. "Everybody wears make-up in vlogs and in life, Millie. It's one of the world's lovely things."

She's gone pale. I can see it even through her foundation.

"Lauren, I don't think no make-up is a bad idea. I want to talk about how you don't want to go online because of how you look. I won't say your name! I'll just talk about how to be more confident and what to do if people call you names. And just by me not wearing make-up, it makes the point that it's real and I believe what I say."

Lauren has gone even paler. There is now probably not even a shade of foundation that exists to match her skin tone.

"Millie, I'm worried about you." Lauren puts her arm round me. "This is basically an invite to every troll in the world. It's like walking up to Mr Style Shame and saying, 'Come into my bedroom and call me a spoon.'"

I remember what Bradley said about everybody getting trolled, whatever they do.

"I can handle it," I say.

At that point, an odd sound starts downstairs. It sounds like a thunderstorm.

Lauren sees me looking a bit concerned.

"Don't worry, Mills. When my dad gets really cross with my mum, he does a drum solo on the radiators with forks. Their marriage counsellor said it was a good way to ease the tension."

I hear Lauren's dad shout, "I'm only here because of her!"

Lauren sighs. "He also does that. A lot."

I don't know what to say. Which is every shade of useless.

Lauren must sense this because she hugs me and says, "Let's get together in the shed tomorrow. Let's do it. I'm there for you every step of the way – as long as I can be off-screen with defined brows and decent lippy."

"I love you, Lauren. You're brilliant. Just please don't marry a Russian dictator."

Rubbish jokes are all I can manage sometimes. She smiles and I leave. Her parents don't notice. Her dad is playing the kitchen units and her mum has turned the TV up to a volume level that even Grandad could hear.

#Help is happening. Lauren is ready. I'm ready. I think.

I think I am. *Can* I handle it though? Can I handle people calling me stuff?

I hope I can delete it from my head.

When I get back to Grandad's, I start to plan what I'm going to say. I write down a few notes. I have to be clear in my head about what I want to say and where I want things to go. I need to keep focusing forward. Moving up like a … lift.

No. You can stop thinking that too. I do NOT fancy Bradley. I do, however, love someone who is just proud to be who they are and gets on with it. Hurrah for escalators … in a way.

#REALVLOGONE

Lauren and I are in the Shed of Vlog. It's Sunday morning and Grandad has taken down his calendar. This is a small but sweet act of loveliness on his part. Now everyone will know we are nothing to do with wading birds.

Lauren moves a spade out of the way and looks at me. "Are you ready, Mills?"

I tell her yes. I've been practising all night in the mirror. I think I've got it. I've planned my advice and how to say it. I've nicked a bit of it from stuff I've seen in magazines but I think I can get away with it.

Lauren counts me in like a proper film director. "Three. Two. One. ACTION!"

"Hello. I'm Millie and welcome to the very first #Help vlog! You can see I'm doing this without any make-up on. Extreme close-up please, Lauren."

(And Lauren zooms the phone RIGHT in so you could basically dive into my pores.)

"And the truth is, I'm really scared. because no make-up means—"

(At this point, we hear a very loud, odd version of "Humpty Dumpty Sat on a Wall".)

"Ignore that! That's my aunty Teresa. She's bought an ice-cream van and she's just got the siren thingy working. She hasn't got any freezers, but she's working on that.

"Um, where was I? OK, I just want to explain why I'm doing this without any contouring or stuff. I love make-up but there are things that are more important than eyeliner. I didn't want to be all shallow and for my vlog just to be about how I look.

"Anyway, today, I want to talk to you about parents. #Help Me Cope With Crazy Adults in My Life. We are always told that anyone over the age of eighteen should know what they are doing. The fact is, they don't. As you can hear, my aunty Teresa has bought a mobile dessert lorry. I wish I could say this was the first crazy thing she's ever done but it's not. And I don't think she's going to change. In fact, as long as the adults in your life are not actually hurting you, you kind of have to accept that they are very unlikely to change. If they are the sort of people who are convinced they invented synchronized swimming in a paddling pool at the age of four, they are probably going to be the same at forty-four.

"Accept them and, if you can, try to help them. For example, my aunty Teresa has said that she is going to make an avocado and chilli ripple ice cream for her van and I've very gently steered her back to peanut butter and caramel. You can make a difference to people's lives and … puddings.

"Now, coping with random adults is less difficult than coping with crazy parents. Crazy parents expect more of you so are basically a different species. I have lovely parents, but my mum is currently going out with a man who thinks that a vacuum cleaner's feelings are worth more than mine. So I'm living with my dad. He is great, but not around that much.

"Generally with parents, I think that the following FOUR things are good to do:

1. Tell them where you are going. If you just disappear somewhere, they get really upset. If your parents watch a lot of programmes like CSI this will be massively the case, as they think really clever murderers live in postboxes on every street.

2. Occasionally – and I know it's hard – start a conversation with them about school. This makes them stupidly happy and they stop asking you all those questions about your day, so it's a massive win-win situation thing.

3. Ask them about what they were like as teenagers. They might be weird about this to start with, BUT you could see a really surprising human side of them. They may have had snogging issues or have been dumped horrifically. Remember, most of them didn't have a mobile phone till they were twenty-something, so their stories can be unbelievable. My mum once waited in a park for over an hour when her friend was meant to be meeting her. Her friend had actually been in a nasty homemade-rollerblade accident in her own garden and couldn't walk. She wasn't horribly injured or anything but no one could tell Mum. Her friend had a hedge

and a wheel on her head and Mum was completely in the dark, sitting in a park eating chips. Our parents had it really tough. You've got to give them a bit of love for that…

4. OK, this step is harder. I have a friend whose parents argue loads but they are staying together because of her. We all know that is just the worst idea ever. It would be far better for them to just call it a day and… Anyway … if you're living with adults who yell a lot, just - I know this is hard - like the HARDEST - but try to remember this is not your fault. And I KNOW they always say that on TV and in books and in serious chats at school. But it's TRUE. Your parents are just tools. A good thing is to take them aside and say, 'Look - your arguing is really getting to me and making me feel awful.' If you tell them how you feel, it might just work. It might not. It could make it worse but honesty's worth a try.

"So that's me, Millie, with #Help Me Cope With Crazy Adults in My Life. Please leave your comments and um … until next time…"

I try to make a hashtag with my hands. I'm not sure it works.

"#Help me to help you!"

Lauren presses stop.

I look at her. "What do you think?" I ask her.

Lauren pulls the sleeves of her shirt over her hands.

"How you say I should handle my parents in real life is different from what you've said there."

This is true. It is.

"I know," I say. "But I'm trying to be more general with things so it can help more people. Do you know what I mean?"

Lauren looks sad. "Yeah," she sighs. "They are pretty unique. In a bad way."

I try to get off the subject and cheer her up. "What did you think of the whole vlog?"

Lauren thinks hard. "Er. Good. For a first go. I think. Not, er, too preachy," Lauren says. "Are you going to upload that?"

She looks unsure. I stare at her.

"You know what, Lauren. I think I'm going to just think about it for a while. I think that's…"

And we both say it together:

"Sensible."

#UPLOAD

I sit in my room for hours. I tidy everything about four times. I look underneath the bed and discover a box of My Little Ponies. I go on eBay to see how much they're worth. I find out they're worth nothing because Teresa has cut off their manes and written, *Teresa is the best jockey ever* all over them. I brush Dave and then try to tie a small bow on her head. She attempts to eat it.

After all this, I still can't decide whether I should upload the vlog or not.

Eventually, I decide I need some advice about my actual advice vlog.

I track down Grandad. He's in his shed. He's put his calendar back up and he's sawing a piece of wood. He does this a lot. You never get to see where the wood goes or what it does.

"Grandad, would you do something even if you thought people would laugh at you for it?"

Grandad stops sawing and sits down. "I married your grandma."

I hate it when he does this. Rubbish, ancient anti-women jokes. You need him to be helpful and he just goes silly.

"Grandad! I'm serious!" I yell.

"So am I," he sighs. "You're old enough now, so I'll tell you something. But keep it to yourself. Your grandma was pregnant with Teresa when I met her."

My brain takes a second or two to process this. This is a major revelation. I had NO IDEA. "What?" I yelp. "So she isn't yours?!"

"She's mine," Grandad says firmly. "Blood isn't always thicker than love. Your grandma was seen as damaged goods years ago. People told me not to marry her. But she was lovely. She'd made a mistake. A man told her he loved her and he didn't. I did. So I married her and I didn't have a miserable day or a sandwich for dinner in thirty-five years. You've got to do what you think is right, Millie. Common sense, that's what you've got. Teresa hasn't got any, but at least she follows her heart. That's something. If YOU think what you've got to say is worth hearing, who cares what other people think? If it could help one person feel better, SHARE IT! But Millie…"

And Grandad looks at me and grabs my hand. "You HAVE to look after yourself though. That's important. Now, get lost. I need to cut some wood."

Grandad may be harsh but sometimes he gets it right.

That's it. I'm going to do it.

I call Lauren as soon as I close the shed door behind me.

"I'm with you," Lauren says and that's JUST what I want to hear. "Can I come over? I'd quite like to get out of the house, and anyway, we're doing this together."

When Lauren arrives at the house, she's carrying a celebratory chocolate hazelnut dip. "Let's toast to our success with sweet breadsticks!" she shouts before shoving one in my mouth and laughing. It's a great friend that helps you AND brings you random sugar.

Just as we are about to press upload, my stomach suddenly goes into a panicked flutter. The questions that have been rushing around my head all day suddenly seem all too real. What am I doing? What will Danny – or Bradley – think about it? What if Mum or Erin see it?

Dave chooses this moment to jump onto my laptop keyboard and attempt to steal a breadstick.

She also presses upload.

Lauren looks at me. "Well, Mills, it's gone. Decision made. It's up. Hashtag it on ALL your accounts with #real #vlog #makeup #feminism #advice #life and anything else that's trending now and let's see what happens!"

I agree with her but tell her we should leave it for twenty-four hours before we even check the views. Otherwise, we'll just get down about it. New vlogs take time to build an audience. I read that in an article.

Lauren just puts her hugely serious face on and says, "This is history, Millie. This is gorgeous Stalin when he could be in a boy band. This is…"

At this point, Aunty Teresa bursts in shouting, "Have you started a proper vlog, Mills?! Grandad mentioned you were doing something involving videos that everyone in the world can see. Brilliant! And perhaps, if it goes viral, you can ever so subtly put an advert in for my ice-cream van too!"

Lauren catches me eye. We don't want to tell Teresa exactly what we've said about her.

"Let's see how it goes," I say.

I think I say this to Aunty Teresa quite a lot.

Aunty Teresa skips off to work on more ludicrous flavours of ice cream.

Lauren looks at me very seriously. "How are you going to even sleep tonight now that it's out THERE?"

My tummy does a backflip. Perhaps I should give my phone to Lauren so I'm not checking it all night, but then … I know that I'll just look at Dad's iPad. It will be impossible not to check. Impossible not to see how people react. Impossible not to… "Loz, it will be impossible."

"Millie!" Lauren shouts. "You're not a celebrity. Nothing will happen for hours. DON'T WORRY. This is a really fun thing we are doing. Don't spoil it!"

Lauren is right but it's a bit of a major life-role reversal when she is the sensible one.

"I bet you can't stop yourself checking it!" I snap.

"Bet I can!" she laughs as she deletes the app off her phone and off mine too.

"Lauren!" I yell. "This is INSANE!" And it is, but I feel like being totally insane.

"RIGHT! No checks till lunchtime tomorrow on any device! #PINKIEPROMISE!" Lauren giggles as she curls her little finger around mine. This is our sacred bond. I can't break this. I think if I do, something dreadful will happen.

It probably won't.

I hope.

I try to have an early night. Dave walks on my forehead pleading with me to give her some tuna-flavoured luxury cat snacks. It's hard to relax.

A MASSIVE part of me says this has been a terrible mistake. It may lead to glory or it may lead to…

#CHEMICALREACTION

I spent last night reading too many articles about terrible diseases. But I managed not to look at the vlog. Now it's Monday morning and I'm sat in Science with Lauren, watching Danny Trudeau.

And I'm not the only one. He's been picked to perform an experiment in front of the class. Never in the history of school anywhere in the world has potassium permanganate been put on a dish so perfectly. The way Danny picks up a spatula is poetry. He follows instructions on the whiteboard with tiny glimpses and, without even looking properly, manages to get just the right amount of scoop. Danny Trudeau. Scoop Master. If this was a YouTube video, the comments section would be all heart emojis and jealous scientists saying they could do it better. They couldn't.

"Mills," whispers Lauren, "he's about to add the glycerine. In a few minutes, we'll see the fire. The true fire of Trudeau."

This makes us both giggle a lot. I don't know what it is but there's something about Danny starting a small chemical explosion that's just about taking my mind off my vlog. It's been itching around in my brain now for hours. All night. ALL day. I am desperate to see how many views we've had. What comments we've got. Who has seen it. Who hasn't seen it. Now I FINALLY have the perfect distraction. Doctor Danny and his spatula of love.

After the lesson, Lauren and me are walking behind the Canadian scientist of dreams and I realize I have the perfect opportunity to talk to him about something clever. I understand everything that just happened. I paid TOTAL attention to all of it. It's like things have all come together to make this one moment. It's like...

It's like Bradley Sanderson is straight in front of my face. Completely blocking the view of Danny's brilliant changing-atoms body.

"I saw it," he says. "I saw your vlog."

There are two problems here. I really want to see Danny but I also want to hear what Bradley thought about the vlog.

"What did you think?" I ask. I try to split my eyes to keep one on him and one on Trudeau's magic. It doesn't work. I just go cross-eyed.

Bradley stares at me hard. "It's really, really ... brave."

I find this a bit worrying. The way Bradley says "brave" doesn't make it feel like a massive compliment. In fact, it makes me feel like I'm doing something really stupid – like riding a bike over a really tall cliff with just a big shirt as a parachute.

Bradley can see my face has slightly collapsed and tries to reassure me. "No. I thought it was like – honest and fresh. I showed my mum and she really liked it."

Lauren nudges me in the ribs and makes "I told you so" eyebrows.

"Great! Mums like it!" My sarcasm explodes with more fizz than Danny's experiment. I feel instantly bad though. Bradley looks almost hurt.

I go all enthusiastic. "How come you saw it? Did you go hunting for it?"

Bradley looks down, sideways, up and everywhere eyes can possibly go. "Er. No. That girl in your year who is always posting on Instagram has shared it."

Lauren and I stare at each other.

Oh no. This is not good.

Danny has stopped to talk to someone. We walk past him. He grins in our general direction. If I wasn't feeling so worried, I could almost think he was smiling JUST at me. But that's the thing about my anxiety – it changes the entire world and how I see everything. He was probably just generally happy at making a small bomb that teachers approve of.

I want to go to the Zen loo and check my phone immediately but I can't. I have to sit through half an hour of Mrs Caldwell going on about binary code. I usually love Mrs Caldwell and her amazing glasses that have interchangeable coloured inserts for different days of the week but I NEED to see what Erin has said.

An Erin take-down could take me down. FOR EVER.

#MEANGIRL

As soon as the lesson ends, I rush to the Zen loo to look at Erin's Instagram. She's posted a link to my vlog and a selfie of herself made up in her usual perfect way. She's tilted her head to the screen, there's metallic on her eyes and the lips are red. It shouldn't work but it's Erin and it does. She's written:

There's a really interesting new vlog called #Help @MilliePorter that basically says people who like make-up are shallow. Girls, I don't think another girl should tell you what you can or can't do. Are you with me? I think it's empowering to use make-up to make the best of your features. If you are anti-make-up, you are anti-freedom, anti-girl and anti-feminist. #feminist #GIRLPOWER #makeup #eyes #lips

I don't even bother to check my vlog. I take the biggest breath it's possible to take, leave the toilets and show it to Lauren. She's standing with Bradley. Lauren puts her arm around me. Bradley puts his arm around me too. What is going on?!

I manage to blurt out, "That's not what I said at all. I just said that—"

"Look, Millie," Bradley says matter-of-factly, despite the fact he's still got his arm around me. "To Erin, you've basically declared war. ANYONE who does anything half decent on social media threatens her. Unless it's about lifts. BUT look, she's given you loads of publicity that you wouldn't have had otherwise."

Bradley is looking at me down his huge glasses in a way that makes me feel a bit confused. He's sweet. And reassuring. And Lauren is looking at us both VERY suspiciously.

"Also, Millie, I, er … wondered to know if you wanted to meet up on Saturday again – to discuss your next vlog?" Bradley continues, going quite red. "I know it doesn't seem like the world of moving staircases and the world of problem-solving have a lot in common but I think, after seeing your … thing … that I know a way you could reach *even more* people."

I can't believe I'm saying this, but I agree and tell Bradley that Saturday sounds lovely. Bradley immediately rushes off doing his usual cling-to-the-wall disappearing act.

After what's happened today, I need all the help I can get. I know I've got Loz, but she's not an expert. And she's currently exploding, grinning from ear to ear.

"Now, Millie," she whispers, "you can't say that is not a date! He totally utterly likes you, NOT JUST IN THE FRIEND WAY! He put his arm around you!"

I go to yell at Lauren about the difference between professional business meetings and dates when Danny Trudeau taps me on the shoulder.

"Hi, Lauren! Hi, Millie! I liked #Help. Nice work! It's good to know that it's not just my family that's crazy. My dad's currently trying to build a model tank from scrap metal. He's been watching too many killer-robot movies and is prepping for their takeover."

I play it cool. "Do you know what sort of tank?"

Danny looks down, shuffles his feet, tilts his head slightly and says, "Kinda big. Grey. Noisy when you're chilling. Are you a weaponry expert, Millie?"

He beams at me. All of a sudden I feel slightly hilarious in the good way.

"Not really. I know a lot about Nerf guns. I can SLAY with a Nerf gun."

Danny looks me square in the face. "Now THAT I would love to see," he says.

There is a huge, drive-a-bus-through-it uncomfortable gap. Am I meant to say, "I would love to have a pretend battle with you!" or "Any time!"?! In the end, just to break the silence, I blurt out, "I'm not really good with Nerf guns. In fact, I've never tried one."

I don't know why I say this. Danny looks a bit sad.

"Anyway," he drawls out, "I'm gonna do what you suggested. Not try to change Dad. Just accept him. Even though he fired a toy grenade at me last night when I was doing my homework! It was a good vlog though. I liked it. Gotta go. Bye, guys."

Once he's gone, Lauren and me look at each other.

"Don't, Millie," Lauren snaps. "You've already got Bradley fancying you. Danny is ERIN PROPERTY. Don't you DARE mess with him. He will be the icing on the cherry."

Lauren means "the icing on the cake". Danny Trudeau is out of bounds. I know it. Lauren knows it. Instagram knows it. THE WORLD knows it.

We hear a lovely clopping sound. Erin swishes by us and breezily calls out, "Hey, Millie! You know I could see what you were trying to do. Something powerful and … real. Only it didn't quite come off, did it? You just looked a bit … tragic. Still, there's time to get good. Keep working on it! Danny, wait!"

And Erin catches up with Danny. I see his face light up. Erin flicks her phone out to show him something. I look at Lauren. Surely they are dating. It is inevitable.

"The Danny cake is burnt, Millie. Move away," Lauren sighs.

The Queen has bagged her prince and I'm Cinderella with a vlog in a shed and no Fairy Godmother.

#COMMENTS

On the way home from school, Lauren and me *finally* read all the comments underneath my vlog. It's had nearly 500 views. Not terrible.

The comments? Er ... mixed.

Good advice ... if you are stupid

This helped with Mum, thanks!

OK, this is a nice person, who deserves a response.

Don't talk about things that you don't understand

OMG pretty gurl

#angst

Bit weird but quite good really

Who do you think you are stupid cow?

Lose 34lbs a week on the Guava Diet

Why are you in a shed? LOL

Respect from Brazil!

Fit. How old are you ;)

Are you a feminist? Is that why you are bare-faced?

I take a few deep breaths.

"Mills! Don't be sad, that's a really good question!" Lauren says.

"Answer that and also say you're not being anti-make-up. You're just saying it's fine not to wear make-up."

Between you and me, I'm feeling a bit flat and angry. Erin has managed to twist everything I've said, ignore the main bit of advice about insane adults and make it somehow all about her. AGAIN.

I start ranting at Lauren. "You know, next time, I will do half of it in make-up and half not and that will shut EVERYONE UP!"

Lauren stops us both dead in the street. "Hang on though. That could be a great idea."

I look at Lauren like she's gone mad. Because she has. "If I do that, EVERYONE will think I'm a complete and utter twonk. Everyone will be talking about it. Everyone..."

Hang on. When you think about it, it's the most perfect way to make my point. This is actually a fantastic idea.

"LAUREN –" I hug her tight – "YOU ARE A GENIUS!" We dance up and down outside Primark for a bit.

Lauren nods her head, looking very proud of herself. "I'll do one side of your face made-up and one side not. You'll look great both ways. Everyone will love you. You will answer Erin without deliberately going for her. Feminism and make-up will be saved. You may even become a sensation."

And then she looks at me while giving it some serious head-swaying sass. "And now you think Bradley is the vlogging BOMB—"

"Well, er, yes, but no, but ... bye, Lauren! See you tomorrow!"

I quickly run away before she can ask me anything more. Perhaps wanting to see Bradley ISN'T just about vlogging. Perhaps I am having major feelings for someone brainy and sweet and perhaps...

When I get to our street, I see that Mum is waiting in Grandad's front porch. She is not looking happy.

It's very easy to lose the ability to talk when my mum is giving the "Stare".

"Millie," she says as she guides and sort of pushes me into the house, "we NEED to talk NOW."

#LECTURE

I take Mum to my bedroom. I've managed to push nearly everything left of Aunty Teresa's underneath the bed. Including her wooden stable and play food that she can't bear to throw out because it reminds her of her first play shop for horses. Not many horses I've met like plastic pizzas, but there is no point arguing with Aunty Teresa.

Mum sits on the end of the bed. "Your dad called me, Millie."

I look at her. That *is* surprising.

"I've heard about this because Grandad told your dad, who told me…" She looks at me and corrects herself. "In fact, I've *seen* you have become one of these people on the Internet who films themselves. And you talked about me and Gary!"

"I didn't!" I shout.

"You spoke about Gary. It's not nice to talk about people behind their backs."

"I didn't say his name, Mum." I sound right AND calm.

"Millie. You know I don't like to be treated like an idiot."

Why, then, is she acting like one by living with one? I can win this argument EASILY.

"Don't worry, Mum," I say quietly, "I'm sure lots of people have got a robot hoover that they treat like a child. No one will realize it's Gary."

Mum gets her strop face on and her voice gets higher. "You also know I don't appreciate sarcasm, Millie. And I'm worried about you. On the Internet, there are evil people pretending to be really nice. They want to hurt you. I mean, do you know who you are talking to? Do you really?!"

I try not to be cross at Dad and Grandad. I try not to be cross at Mum. She is patronizing me to death but I know it's because she loves me so I keep calm.

"Mum, seriously! I am talking *to them*. They are not talking to me. I don't say where I live. Not even the country I come from. I know what I'm doing."

Mum's face goes red. "Does it make you a target for really terrible people though, Millie?"

I still keep calm. "I think you've been watching too many films with Liam Neeson, Mum. Honestly, I promise if I had any worries, I would come to you. I always have, haven't I? Like that time when someone at school told me that Father Christmas took all your teeth away if you'd been naughty that year. I was sleeping face down all December. Remember?"

"Well," Mum says, "to use that story, these Internet people, like Father Christmas, are basically coming down the chimney and they—"

There! I knew she was going to overreact! I have to shut her down before I lose it.

"Mum. Honestly. I'm fine. And all the homework's still being done."

And it is – I make time. I've got time. I still haven't got an actual desk in this house but I just use Aunty Teresa's TV-dinner *Despicable Me 2* tray.

"Oh Millie…" Mum sounds a bit sad now. "I'm missing out on what you do. Come home. I know I can't make you. Please just remember I AM HERE. ALWAYS. ALWAYS."

And she does her heart fist pump, where she bangs her chest and then pats it on mine.

This makes me want to cry.

My mum is lovely really. I know I should be hating on her, and loads of my friends don't get on with their mums, but mine is cool. Apart from the fact she's going out with a really clean dictator. Like a lemon-fresh Stalin.

If you love someone, it's often better if you have different houses. It just sorts it ALL out. I may do a vlog on it.

"By the way," Mum asks me as we go downstairs, "where is your dad?"

"Oh, he's out doing some work."

Between you and me, I have absolutely no idea where he is.

#HONEST

After Mum's gone, I feel a bit down. It doesn't help that it's Monday, when you just feel like you've got so far to go till the weekend.

If I was doing an honest vlog tonight, this is what I would really talk about:

1. Those comments really hurt. They sting inside and make me feel sick. I KNOW they shouldn't, but they do. And I want to keep the vlog going so Erin and all the haters don't win. BUT IT'S HARD.

2. My dad is never here! Grandad acts more like my dad. I see Dave the cat more than I see my own father – and she's always out doing the feline party thing. I know Dad loves having me here but it's just like my mum said: Dad is completely … his own man. He's not a bad man. He's not a bad dad. If I was in trouble, I know he would be here for me. But in normal life, he just lets me get on with things and he does his own thing and I…

3. OK, I'm only telling you this. I sort of miss a clean home and knowing people are going to be around when they say they will be. I don't miss McWhirter

and being treated like an actual ball of fluff on laminate wood flooring CONSTANTLY. But I do miss all the … organization. The stuff that makes you feel safe and not … panicky. I AM SO DULL. If only Gary "Neat Freak" Woolton would DO ONE and take his specialist flat screen anti-static wipes somewhere else.

4. I love Danny Trudeau and I've got no chance. And this isn't me wanting you to say, "Of course you have, Millie!" in a fish-for-compliments special, because if you've seen Erin, you'd know what I mean. ZERO chance.

5. If all that wasn't enough, I'm confused about Bradley Sanderson. I didn't want to admit it to Lauren, but I think I like him. In what way, I don't even know. I need the sensible part of my head to detach from all this squiggled-spoon-confused bit and sort it out. Or I could tell Mum. But that would mean admitting I can't really cope and that I'm not that … clever. Or wise. Or anything my vlog claims.

So that's my honest vlog. But there's no way I want to share all this with the rest of the world right now. Just you and Dave the cat. Who is currently halfway up the curtain swinging from side to side. To her, a curtain is just a fabric playground. She's probably only copying what Aunty Teresa has already done anyway.

#MAKEOVER

"Millie. Just admit it. You're going on a date with Bradley Sanderson at the weekend."

The Monday blues have gone and now it's #Help night. Lauren and me are just about to do another vlog (even though this makes my heart race). I also think Lauren might have realized I'm finding the whole Bradley thing confusing. I'm not telling her that though.

"It's NOT a date, Loz. Like the last one was not a date. It's a ... meeting about how I can improve my marketing strategy."

"Come on, Millie." Lauren looks at me like she doesn't believe a word I'm saying. "It's seriously about YOU liking him. If you two had babies, they would be like the most clever sensible babies in the world. They could be like ... Mark Zuckerberg."

I can't handle this level of Lauren love talk, so I go factual instead. This is a great way to get her off her current track of randomness.

"Loz, did you know you can change your language to 'Pirate' on Facebook?"

This is old news but I've hooked her in. We never use Facebook these days, so I could tell her anything. I can see Lauren's brain has gone into serious overdrive.

"Really, Millie? Why?"

"I don't know," I say. "The point is, I'm not having babies with Bradley Sanderson. He's got a girlfriend in the States he's never met."

"But why would anyone want to talk like a pirate?" Lauren is looking in real brain pain now.

My slightly evil plan has worked. Lauren has been diverted by fact.

"Let's get prepared and do the vlog."

We spend the next two hours doing make-up and it's magnificent. One side of my face has Erin-based levels of cosmetic PERFECTION. On the other side, there is NOTHING. I look like a spoon but a spoon with a FANTASTIC POINT.

Lauren counts me in and I go OFF!

"Hello! Millie Porter here with #Help! This time #Help Me To Cope with Make-Up. Can I be a feminist and wear make-up? Well, I've done something a little bit special with the help of my BFF Lauren that I just want to share with you.

"I've done my face like this…"

(I thrust my make-up perfection side into the camera.)

"And half of it like this…"

(I show the entire world my bare face.)

"The point is, wear make-up or don't wear make-up. Both are great. YOU can do what you like. Feminism is not about eyeliner or what we look like. It's about us being judged on who we really are. It's about us not getting treated differently because we are girls. It's about us getting the same opportunities as men whether we have smoky eyes or bare eyes. It's about my grandad not assuming that I can cook because I'm female. I can't and I don't want to. Well - I might want to when I'm older but only because I have decided I want to make something nice for ME that isn't baked beans. And that's the point - make-up is ABOUT DOING IT FOR YOU! Like making your lunch! You aren't doing it to please men. They don't even understand decent contouring. Generally...

"The world these days HAS evolved. Like dinosaurs. Well, not like dinosaurs, as they died out. Probably because they didn't embrace feminism.

"Anyway, LOOK - basically, if you're wearing make-up and having fun, brilliant - you're a feminist.

"If you're NOT wearing make-up and having fun, congratulations, you're a feminist too!"

(At this point, I flash my face from side to side again, so everyone gets the full effect of the make-up.)

"Thank you. Leave any comments underneath. #Help me to help you! Loving your work!"

Lauren gives me a massive thumbs up.

"Mills! That was really good. I mean, the bit about the dinosaurs was a bit random but it sort of worked. Perhaps it wasn't a massive comet that wiped them out. Perhaps it was all the female stegosauruses killing off the male T-Rexes in anger at their sexism and it all just escalated and—"

"It was definitely a comet, Loz," I say. "Let's upload it. The world needs to see your make-up genius." I can't believe I'm just going for it.

Lauren stares at me. "Yes, the world does, Millie, but you do need to wash it off before your whole family think you've completely lost it."

Yet again, we've done the sensible swaps. What is happening to me?

#TROLLS

I wake up early the next day. It's difficult sleeping at the moment because I can't wait to look at what's happened to the vlog. In fact, I do check it a few times in the night because the South American crew are a bit behind us time-wise and I just want to see if not speaking Spanish or Portuguese makes a difference to my message.

Who am I kidding? This is a fight for school subscribers. Not for global supremacy.

The good news is … my subs are growing. Over 300. And I've had over 452 views. Erin gave me the most excellent piece of advertising ever by having a major dig at me.

The bad news is … the comments. They are mainly horrible.

I have two pet dinosaurs that aren't getting on. What do you suggest?

(OK, actual LOL!)

Dweeb. Dog.

You think you're cool. What you know? Dweeby Dog.

Cute idea! Nice vlog ☺

Of course feminism is about how you look! Please leave intelligent things to the grown-ups

I bet Germaine Greer and Caitlin Moran are quaking in their boots!

(I think this is sarcastic.)

Only ugly girls are feminists

(CAN YOU BELIEVE PEOPLE LIKE THIS EVEN EXIST?! TROLL!)

Offensive to REAL feminists

Ugly girl moans about men. Same old same old

You're ugly whatever. Put bag over head!

OK. That one does really, really get to me. I look in the mirror. No, I'm not Erin Breeler standard (who is?) but I'm not ugly either. And so what if I was?! It's like what J. K. Rowling said about fat people – is fat really the worst thing we can be? Is ugly? It's not. It's worse to be a nasty piece of work who goes out to make people feel horrible about themselves.

That isn't what J. K. Rowling said exactly by the way. She said it better, but…

Ugly?

It HURTS. And I can't stop thinking about it. And the sensible side of me thinks it's just some troll spreading the hate but this HUGE side of me says all this vlogging is a terrible idea and Mum is completely right and I'm completely wrong.

Why would you write that stuff? I mean, why would you go out to make someone feel bad about themselves when they have done nothing to you whatsoever?

I call Lauren first thing in the morning.

"Have you seen the comment that says I'm ugly?"

"Oh Mills! That is TOTALLY just a troll. Look at all the other comments! There are some NICE ones on there too. What would you say to me? Don't focus on the spoon! Look at all the other shiny, lovely cutlery drawer things!"

This is true. My sensible self is returning. "What should I do next, Loz?"

Lauren's voice slightly collapses. "To be honest, Mills, I've got quite a lot to think about myself at the moment. After I got home last night, my dad accused my mum of fracking an entire cheesecake."

I'm trying to make a great vlog and I need Lauren's help. AND what she's saying makes no sense. I snap at her a bit. "Fracking as in when you mine for gas and stuff?"

"Yeah!" Lauren sighs sadly. "He said she ate it like an industrial process. He just knows what will really wind her up. The way she looks, the way she snores, the way she eats…"

I try to get her back on what we are talking about. My vlog. Me getting trolled into trolldom and beyond. We both know we can't fix her parents.

"You realize what your biggest problem is, Millie? It's Erin. I heard from lovely Gracie yesterday that Erin's thinking of launching a style vlog. If you ask me, that's definitely a revenge vlog attack. Anyway, see you at school in a bit."

As soon as I'm off the phone to Lauren, I check Erin's Instagram. Sure enough, she's posted the most gorgeous selfie ever with:

NEWS of an exciting new partnership with some people I KNOW you will love. Plus, something you've always wanted! And I promise it's not going to involve garden sheds ;) It's just going to be COMMITTED TO GORGEOUS #ComingSoon

Her friend Miranda has commented:

Can't wait, E! Will make a change from some DULLSVILLE preachy channels ;)

This feels like a war now. I don't want it to be a war. I want it to be a peace. A big piece of peace. Perhaps Bradley will have some suggestions about what to do. There must be rival escalator vlogs that want to bring him down. That wasn't meant to be a bad up-down joke by the way. Even though it was. Sorry.

#DATE

Meeting Bradley in the shopping centre on Saturday again starts off sort of weirdly.

We meet by his favourite lift and the first thing I notice is that he's looking really good. And the fact I think he looks good takes me by surprise. He's got a Star Wars T-shirt on with a jacket and it sort of works. "I was going to do the full cosplay Vader on you." He smiles. "But I decided committed dark side isn't really your style."

This makes me giggle. "The truth is, Bradley, if you want to turn up as FULL Jedi Knight, I don't really care."

Bradley sort of spins from side to side and laughs. "Surely you wouldn't want me to be Yoda."

"At least Yoda is wise," I say. I like Yoda. I don't know much about Star Wars but I know he talks a lot of sense.

"So you'd prefer your men, Millie, to be two foot tall, old, green and to talk in object–subject–verb word order?"

I stare at him hard. "I'll be honest, Bradley. I don't know what you mean."

"Nor do I really," Bradley admits. "I looked it up on Wikipedia. I've noticed if you tell people things you've read on Wikipedia with a really straight face, everyone thinks you are really clever. For example, did you know that people with blue eyes are much more likely to have an accident involving trousers that don't fit properly than people with brown eyes?"

"Really?" This is an amazing statistic and one I could use in a vlog. It's good advice for getting dressed.

"It's totally made up," Bradley says. "I've also noticed that people believe everything I say because I'm a smart nerd with glasses."

This is actually really quite funny. I laugh and see Bradley crack a tiny smile. It's sweet.

"Tell you what is true." Bradley goes serious again. "More people die from taking selfies than are eaten by sharks."

"Honestly?" I squeal. "Wow. What would happen if sharks got the ability to take selfies themselves?"

Bradley thinks hard. "I suppose fatalities would rocket because people would take a selfie with a shark because it was cool and then they'd be eaten."

This is the most bizarre conversation I've had in a very long time (and my BFF is Lauren) but I am really enjoying it.

Bradley and me go for a coffee. I let him pay this time. It's only fair. And this time, he's not mansplaining to me either. It's a conversation between equals. It's…

Why am I being so defensive over Bradley?

Once we've sat down, I ask the question I really want to ask: "How often should I be uploading? I've done two vlogs in a week now."

"You should upload as much as you want to. There is such a thing as too much though. I do it every week. It builds up a bit of excitement, especially if I'm featuring a speciality piece of machinery."

This conversation has gone odd. I feel like I can say anything to him, like I can with Lauren. My mouth ends up blurting out, "I've had a few people saying bad stuff. Like I'm ugly."

Bradley brushes my arm for a millisecond to make the point, looks at me and very gently says, "That is trolling, Millie. I did warn you."

And then it goes even MORE weird, so Bradley starts talking really quickly.

"But more to the point, you are funny and interesting and it's something different from the endless girl stuff. I loved your last vlog. I am so OVER girl stuff. Pinky cheeks, eyebrows, princess castles. UNICORNS WITH GOLD-TINGED MANES – WHAT IS IT ALL ABOUT?"

"You don't have to watch it, Bradley," I snap, glad to change the subject. "And a lot of girls don't like it either AND, even if we do – AND I DO A BIT – it's not what we're all about. We can like what we like anyway. There's no such thing as boy stuff or girl stuff! There's just STUFF!"

Bradley looks down. "Well, I've lost people I love to make-up. Like me and my American girlfriend. We were drifting apart, so I've decided we should probably call it a day. Better to do it before we met in real life. She was always a bigger cosplayer and now she's not so into the fun side of it. I don't care about the sort of lipstick that Captain Marvel would wear. She can fly! She can shoot energy bursts from her hands! She can do hand-to-hand combat! I don't think she is going to nip into Boots in the middle of fighting evil and ask for a consultation."

Bradley is angry. And also very funny.

"I'm sorry about your girlfriend." I have to say something. He looks really sad.

"Well, that's the way it goes." Bradley sighs. "Long-distance stuff is always hard. Anyway, you're different. You understand that it's not just about how you look. It's BRAINS too. BRAINS. I like brains. I like talking about stuff that's actually interesting. Not just lifts. THE WORLD. I'm a feminist, you know."

Bradley then looks really seriously at me. "Do you like flapjacks or cupcakes?" he asks.

This question catches me by surprise. It's not often you go from superheroes to sponges.

"Flapjacks."

"I knew you would." Bradley does the loveliest smile a lift-loving cosplay geek vlogger could ever do. "I knew you wouldn't be taken in by all that icing. Now you know what you should do in your next vlog? Talk about trolling and how to deal with it. Talk about how it made you feel. That's REAL. Talk about the hard stuff, Millie."

I am enjoying this afternoon far more than I thought I would. I knew I'd get a lot from it in a professional way but I didn't expect to get into random conversations about long-distance relationships, the way people change and cakes. It's weirdly very natural and easy.

#FLAPJACKGEEKLOVE

That night starts with a Lauren love conspiracy theory.

"You are SO in love with Bradley Sanderson it's not even true."

I've told her about my afternoon at the shopping centre and her response is very predictable.

"Lauren, this is going to shock you but it *is* possible to be with a boy and not snog him. But he was lovely. He's funny. He was talking about sharks and what would happen if they got mobile phones!"

Lauren stays quiet.

I try to explain a bit more. "Yes. You had to be there but he's sweet and he looked really good. Nice jacket. A Star Wars shirt that actually he—"

Lauren interrupts. "Millie – I'm sorry but this man is in love with you. You're so vlog-obsessed these days, you can't see the OBVIOUS that's right in front of your eyes. Well, if you don't fancy him, you should be careful not to go all Erin about him and mess with his feelings."

This feels rather like Lauren is attacking me so I go a bit mad and say, "Lauren. He is NOT in love with me. No more than Danny is, so get that STRAIGHT out your head!"

This is very snappy for me and I feel nervous. Lauren and me, we don't really argue. I think we can both sense it's getting a bit heavy. There's a pause. I'm worried about what she's going to say next. Even the *thought* of a row with Lauren makes me want to throw up.

Then Lauren says, "Are you going cosplay on me? I don't mind but, if you are, can you warn me? Because if I come round here and you're dressed up like something from *The Walking Dead*, it could properly freak me out."

This makes me smile. This is proper Lauren.

"Why would I go zombie on you, Loz?"

"I don't know," she says. "I just have seriously bad zombie nightmares. Hashtag that time my dad dressed up for Halloween and took the barbecue-sauce-over-his-head thing a bit too far. Even now, any hint of a chipotle dressing and I seriously feel vom. Anyway, you're now going out with a cosplayer—"

"I'm not!" I yell. "He's just my … media advisor!"

And we both collapse laughing at this, because clearly I'm not a massive celebrity vlogger and I do not need any sort of advisor in anything.

While we giggle, Bradley messages me.

Thank you for giving me the time today. Can we do it again soon? We can discuss how we can stop aquatic predators with very sharp teeth getting hold of the latest technology. Imagine sharks with Tasers. B

Bradley uses the kind of words I use and he's very clever.

Lauren asks me who's messaged me. I lie and say Gracie.

I have to. It would get too complicated otherwise.

"Let's do a vlog in a bit, Loz. Why don't you stay over?"

After my time with Bradley, I'm totally fired up about doing another vlog. He's RIGHT. I need to FOCUS. Tackle the trolls.

Lauren looks really pleased. "Great idea, Mills! I'll just call my mum and tell her I won't be back this evening. To be honest, I don't think she'll notice, but then, you never know! Meet you in #Help Global HQ."

This is a very sweet way of describing Grandad's ever so slightly mouldy shed.

#KEBAB

I skip down to the shed to find Grandad is just closing the door. He's carrying an old jam jar full of nails. He has lots of these. They are a bit like his pieces of wood. He never seems to use them.

He grunts at me. "Must be going well, Millie. Don't you let fame go to your head though."

It's hardly fame, Grandad, but then he still doesn't understand how to use the Sky Plus. I'm not even going to try to begin to explain this.

"I don't understand it, Millie," Grandad continues. "But Teresa tells me it's going well. It's going better than her attempts to make a smoky-lamb-flavoured ice cream anyway."

"Do you ever get annoyed at Teresa, Grandad?" This is sort of a mean thing to ask but I do wonder. Grandad is old-fashioned and sensible and Teresa is … not.

Grandad stares at me. He looks tired. "You have to let people make their own choices, Millie. Some people think I should have been harder on my kids and then they both wouldn't be living at home with me and trying to make money in stupid ways. But there are more things to life than making money and having a job that impresses people. It's called contributing, Millie. Contributing."

What does this mean? I hope I'm not going to get a gardening lecture. It was lovely of Grandad to help me out with my pumpkin competition in Year 2 but I know far too much about rhubarb than the average thirteen-year-old should.

"Contributing to other people's lives. Trying to make things better. There's lots of ways to do it. Collecting the rubbish is a way to contribute. Just looking after yourself is a way to contribute. Even trying to fuse a kebab and a Cornetto is a way to contribute to life. You are doing it by sharing that common sense of yours and trying to make people's lives better. I'm proud of you."

This makes me so warm inside I could burst. Compliments from Grandad are like really rare orchids that only grow in specific climates.

I told you. I know far too much about plants.

"But just one thing, Millie." Grandad looks almost stern. "I know that brain of yours. Full of ideas but full of worries too. Don't give so much away of yourself that you've got nothing left. Don't get into situations that put you in the firing line of idiots. You're still only young. You may have an old head on those shoulders but it's a sensitive head that needs watering, shelter and love. Keep away from the weeds. And remember, sometimes weeds have pretty flowers."

I give him a hug.

"Now I suppose you'll be wanting my shed again. Well, you can have it. I've got a serious appointment with some begonias out the front."

"Thanks, Grandad."

I love Grandad. I suppose getting trolled is as inevitable as getting your fingernails muddy when you do the gardening. You just have to toughen up and get a good liquid soap. Or something. You can't wash bad thoughts away but you can park them in the furthest bit of the brain supermarket car park near the mind petrol station.

I really need to get my head together before the next vlog or no one will actually know what on earth I'm talking about.

#TROLLTAKEDOWN

Lauren plods into the shed. Her eyes look a bit red. She must have been using her witch hazel wipes to redo her mascara. She squishes her face up, holds up her make-up bag and points at me. "Now. Do you want some foundation just to make you look a bit less like actual Death?"

Before I have the chance to say anything, a brush is on my face.

I very gently move Lauren's hand away. "No. Let's keep it natural and real and ... us."

Lauren squeals. "Mills! I've just got a massive splinter from the shed."

Lauren shows me her finger. There is literally a tree sticking out of it.

"Lauren! That looks terrible! Have you had a tetanus jab? It's this disease that's in plants and wood and stuff. It makes your whole body lock up. You can't speak or anything!"

It's amazing how many things can kill you horribly. Even sweet things like blades of grass and daisies. And mushrooms. There is a type of mushroom that basically makes your liver explode. It's called a death cap. There's also a destroying angel. It sounds like something out of a horror film but it can grow in forests near your house. This is why I like living in a town. These are the sorts of things that I wish I didn't know. My head goes a bit odd and my breathing feels…

"So tetanus locks up your entire body? If only Erin would get it!" Lauren giggles.

This is an evil thing to say but it stops my brain spiralling down in fungus doom.

Lauren looks guilty. "Well, I don't want her to die but it would be nice if she could shut up for a time. Though knowing her, if she got tetanus, her face would freeze in a massive beautiful grin and she'd take a selfie from the hospital and get a million likes."

This is probably true but I say to Lauren, "Let's just get your splinter out."

"OH!" Lauren leaps in the air! "Shall we film it?! Shall we do like a first-aid advice thing? Medical procedures get loads of views and stuff and we – OUCH!"

It's out.

Lauren looks really disappointed. "We really missed an opportunity there, Mills. Splinter vlogging could be massive. Do you want me to give myself another one so we can film it?"

"No, Lozza! That's crazy. Don't hurt yourself! Let's just do my vlog."

"Do you know what you're going to say?"

The truth is, I have a very good idea because I haven't been thinking of a lot else.

"Yeah. I've got a rough idea," I mumble.

The thing is, after talking with Bradley, I now know there are people waiting to hear what I'm going to say. They'll get alerts when I post. Their phone will ding! Or beep! Or vibrate!

I take a deep breath. Lauren gets out of shot and sticks her thumb up.

"Hello! Millie Porter here! #Help Me Cope with Trolling.

"I'm just going to read you some of the comments that have been left on my vlog recently.

'Talentless ugly cow. Delete your account.'

'Why bother???? Fat and not funny.'

'Typical woman telling us how to act. Sort your own life out.'

'Ugliest fake ever.'"

(Reading them out again makes the sides of my eyes feel itchy. Got to keep bright. Got to keep sensible. I swallow.)

"It's really hard to read stuff like that but here's what I try to remember. These people don't know me. They're just really sad, horrible people sat in their bedrooms or at bus stops with no friends. And they probably feel dreadful and useless about themselves. If they see someone doing something fun or interesting, they just want to hurt them and bring them down.

"I'm not saying I think you should be nice to trolls. Just ignore them or imagine them standing in a shopping centre in their underpants. That's what my mum does before big meetings and it makes even scary people totally silly. Focus on the good stuff or the nice comments instead.

"We can all be tools. I'm not saying it's right! I'm saying inner toolness can erupt like a volcano and spew spoon magma all over your … shirt. Like that project I did in primary school.

155

"Anyway, SERIOUSLY, bullying is horrible and it makes your life a living misery. It could be names or slaps. It could be to your face or online or ALL of that. The point is, don't take it. Tell someone IN POWER because you deserve to be feeling ... good. No one should feel rubbish because of other people. I KNOW that sounds preachy and dorky but look, it is FACT. Just like it is a fact that you can't lick your elbow. Look!"

(And I try to lick my elbow.)

"And I know you're probably looking at me now thinking, she looks like a massive spoon with no make-up, but that just goes to show that looks can be – what's the word? – a bit wrong and um ... just ... just ... don't think that you're on your own. You are NOT.

"So that's me, Millie. #Help me to help you and leave any comments below. Unless you're a troll. You can hashtag OFF!"

It sounds good. I'm pleased. Then I hear an odd noise in the background. It's my best friend and she is crying.

I rush over to hug her. "Lauren. What's the matter?"

Lauren sniffs. "Oh, it's just you talking about not letting other people bring you down. It makes me think of my mum and dad. I spoke to my mum, Mills, and she said I'm not allowed to stay, but you know, I honestly dread going home. What's the point of me being there? It's like when I had that piñata for my birthday and my mum started smashing it in a temper. There were Haribo gummy bears everywhere. I know that sounds sort of funny now but it wasn't. The thing is, Mills—"

At this precise, dreadful point to burst in, Aunty Teresa bursts in and says, "HELLO, GIRLS! Oh! Lauren, are you OK? It's boys, isn't it? Don't worry, I get it. Boys do make you cry. The fact is, they don't mature till they're about twenty-three and honestly, they're not worth crying about. Is it kissing? It's difficult, isn't it? The best thing to do is practise on your own hand. Just stick your tongue out and kind of—"

"Teresa! We don't need to hear this right now!" I yell.

Teresa actually shuts up. For four seconds.

"OK. I'm going, but if you want to know ANYTHING about boys, just come to me. I am your woman for any information about men and ice cream. They are very similar things. Nice but they melt under pressure. And you—"

"TERESA!" I find myself properly yelling in a way that is slightly out of control and hurts my throat. Teresa just nods her head and dashes out of the shed.

I look at Lauren. I don't really know what to say.

"Sorry!" Lauren sniffs. "It's just … all very hard. Anyway, listen, I'd better get home. It will only make it worse if I'm late."

I give Lauren a hug and we go back inside. She grabs all her stuff from my room and says a slightly teary goodbye.

I can't imagine what it must be like going home to actual war. I know what it's like going home to total neatness and now total chaos, but THAT. The only really horrid stuff in my life is trolling but at least that's the outside world. It must be horrible if your family aren't there for you. You need to look after the people you love.

My mind feels so full at the moment. There's the vlog and there's

157

Erin and Bradley and Danny and Lauren's parents and Gary and the trolls and my head is spiralling a tiny bit…

My chest feels like someone is sitting on it.

That's when I decide to call my mum.

#MUM

Mum answers the phone almost immediately. She's on hands-free in the car and turns down her awful music.

"Hello, darling," she says. "What's up?"

What is up? Where to start? I can't, so I just say, "I want to tell you I love you."

Mum pauses and says, "That's good."

Then there's a massive uncomfortable silence and I find myself blurting out, "Have you had a tetanus job lately, Mum?"

Mum sounds puzzled. "Er … no. The advice has changed. You only have to… I'm not sure. We order the needles but I'm not a doctor, darling. If I ever start working with animals from abroad, I'll have one."

Despite working in a hospital, Mum always gets tetanus mixed up with rabies.

Mum starts to sound worried. "Millie, have you been reading about tropical diseases on Wikipedia again?"

I can't lie to my mum.

"No… Well, a bit. Tetanus isn't tropical though. It's here."

"Hang on. I'm pulling over. What's really the problem, Millie?

What are you worried about? I know how your head works."

And she does know. She gets me better than anyone. I just can't tell her right now.

I don't say a word and Mum says, "Come home whenever you want. You know you can. We miss you."

It's like she's psychic.

"I know," I say to her. "Anyway, you get on. I just love you."

"I love you too, Millie – and just before you go … if you ARE feeling worried about something, make a list of all the things that are on your mind. It really helps and you can work through them one by one. It's the sensible thing to do. See you soon. Love you. Bye!"

I flop back on my bed. The truth is, I'm worried about LOTS of things. And I KNOW some of them are silly and stupid but I can't help myself. I'm doing an advice vlog, but inside I'm a mess.

1. My best friend may be getting tetanus.
2. My mum could possibly have tetanus too for all I know. She doesn't understand things she should understand – like deadly diseases.
3. I have made the worst enemy on earth in Erin…
4. I have a massive crush on a boy who will never be mine.
5. A boy who Erin really likes too and who really likes Erin.
6. There are really bad people on the news doing really bad things.
7. What if the bad people get hold of terrible mushrooms?
8. OK, that one is ridiculous. Perhaps these lists do help.
9. Am I hurting my mum by not being with her?
10. Where is my dad?

11. Will Aunty Teresa actually kill someone with her fusion food?

12. Please let Aunty Teresa never put mushrooms in food.

13. Sometimes I worry that terrible things are happening to the people I love and there's NOTHING I can do about it.

14. People are calling me ugly and it hurts.

15. My vlog just makes me look like a massive dork.

16. My vlog just makes me sound like a massive dork.

At that point, I get a text.

```
Millie. Had a great idea about your vlog.
Promise not to cosplay too much. Want to meet?
```

I hadn't even replied to his last text. I add another point to the list.

17. I STILL don't know how I feel about Bradley.

I upload the vlog. It's 7.45 p.m. I will honestly, HONESTLY not check the vlog again till 7 a.m. tomorrow…

#HEART

I wake up at 4 a.m. on Sunday morning. This is just plain wrong. This time should not exist. I've had more views on the vlog than on the previous one. I give in and check the comments.

I watched your vlog. It's not as easy as that.

You look fresh! I love your look! It makes a change from everyone else covered in lipstick.

SPOON.

Trolls aren't all tragic. Some of us genuinely hate you.

Perhaps I've taken on too much. I can't *really* tackle stuff that I haven't experienced myself, can I? I do just sound stupid and dorky. People have told me I'm a spoon and do you know what? They're right. I better think hard about what I can vlog about next. Like Bradley says, I have to think about my brand.

But then there's one comment from DanTruds1290…

Another great vlog.

And a heart emoji.

A HEART!!! THAT'S EPIC.

And confusing.

Does that mean he…?

Danny and Bradley are in my head a lot. Like a massive swirling boy mess. My whole body feels like a whirlwind. I need to try and go back to sleep.

#MILLSTHESPILLS

I'm dreading school this week. I know full well that another vlog puts me right in the Erin bombing range and I don't know how to respond to Danny's heart. It might just be a friendly heart or it might be a big pulsating "LET'S BE TOGETHER" heart.

No prizes for guessing which one Lauren thinks it is. When we are looking for a table in the canteen at lunch, I tell her about the heart.

"He could just be being friendly," Lauren says grumpily. This isn't really the answer I wanted to hear. She's been grumpy all morning.

"You don't know that for sure!" I say.

"Oh, come on, Millie," Lauren almost snaps at me. "You know Danny and Erin are spending LOADS of time together. Stop being greedy! Bradley is your man! He's a major full-on nerd and you are pretty with a mega brain. You went on a date. Do the love maths."

The truth is, I think she may be right. He did look at me down his glasses the same way he looks at escalators. With love and respect. "But do I want to have a relationship with someone who spends all their time in lifts?"

"Lifts are sexy!" Lauren says with her big wide eyes looking a bit annoyed. "In films, people always kiss in lifts because they're private, aren't they? You could even combine vlogs! #Help From an Escalator."

This makes me laugh LOTS. "Lauren … don't be ridicu—"

What happens next will go down in history.

While I'm laughing, I seem to completely lose the ability to actually walk. My right leg decides it would like to break free of my body and make a dash for the other side of the room. I find myself flying through the air. In slow motion. I slam my hands down to break my fall but my tray and my food fly absolutely everywhere. I basically create a chip fountain. It's probably spectacular to watch.

The whole canteen erupts into clapping and cheering. This is normally what happens when someone drops their tray but it's probably the most embarrassing thing that has ever happened to me EVER.

Lovely Gracie runs over and starts helping me pick up the chips. Lauren picks me up. She gets falling over. "It's hormonal," she whispers. "We can't help it. It causes an ankle and toe imbalance. Even without high heels. Remember when I did it? It's a normal part of life."

From the corner of my eye, I see Danny staring at me.

Way to go, Millie. There's nothing like a good carpet of carbohydrate when you are trying to impress the man of your dreams.

I also see Erin. The grin is wide and the phone is UP. She got all the aftermath.

Also RUNNING towards me is Bradley with another plate of

food. How did he get that so quickly? He must be sacrificing his own chips.

"Here you are, Millie!" he says. "Saves you queuing again."

I know where that photo is going to end up too.

Erin has double missiles now. "The Fall" and what she would term "The Dweeb Save". She certainly doesn't approve of someone like Bradley. He's got the following but he's not got any cool in her opinion.

I brush myself down and slink into a chair as quickly as I can. Things get back to normal in the canteen quite quickly but in my head there's a big, really bad music festival of Erin and people's mouths yelling and laughing and staring and pointing and noise and…

Breathe. I just have to take deep breaths and BREATHE.

"Mills, are you all right now?"

Lauren knows the answer to this question is "No" but she isn't sure what to do about it. Her asking "Are you all right?" is kind of her saying, "Please be OK" and "I don't know what to do to make you feel better."

I tell her I'm fine but my heart is racing and I feel dizzy and sick and like I might explode. Of course I'm not fine. What just happened is embarrassing in a terminal way.

When he's actually around, my dad *still* talks about things that happened to people at school, and he's ancient. He can't remember his credit card PIN number but he can tell you about the time Nicholas Clarkson's swimming trunks floated to the top of the swimming pool before Nicholas Clarkson did. He was called "Nudey Nick" for SEVEN years after that. My dad still calls him it. To my dad he'll *always* be "NUDEY NICK, NUDEY NICK, YOUR BARE BOTTOM MAKES US SICK." They even made up a song for him.

Now I'll be Mills … MILLS THE SPILLS. It even rhymes! "Mills the Spills, Mills the Spills, with her dropped-chip-lunch coolness she kills." I will be called this for ever. Even when I'm forty-three and living in…

Breathe, Millie. Breathe. That's what I have to say to myself.

It's at times like this that my mum rushes into my head and says, "Millie, you're fine. You're OK. You're OK." It's like she's chanting it. She's done it in real life and she does it in my brain when I need her to.

Eventually, I feel the feeling come back to my face a bit. My second lunch has gone very cold and I just push it away. I feel bad rejecting Bradley's chips but I've lost my appetite completely. My mouth isn't working but my eyes are. Erin has squeezed next to Danny and they are giggling. I know what will happen now…

#ENJOYYOURTRIP

Later on, as we're walking home from school, Lauren checks her phone.

"You're on Mr Style Shame, Mills. But that was pretty inevitable, really. Anyone in the canteen could have sent him that photo. And it's not got THAT many likes."

I don't really know how I feel about this. "Check Erin's account, Loz."

"Millie! She's got over 9,000 followers now. And there are loads of photos of her and Danny. They do look really good together."

This feels a bit much. I death-stare Lauren. "I know. I've seen them."

"Oh! She's also posted a photo of all your spilled chips and the smashed plate! But the caption is actually really nice. Look! Why would she do that?"

I read what Erin has written.

Don't you just love that feeling you get when you see two people who are just meant to be together? Today at school a girl fell over and dropped her lunch tray and a lovely boy helped her up #ChipRomance #GeekLove. I heart seeing people who might

not be lucky enough to have loads of friends being kind to other people who really do need #Help #HeartWarming

"You see," Lauren says. "That's actually really lovely."

Lauren has completely missed the evil point. "So it's kind to say someone really needs help and is less fortunate than you?"

"I've heard you say things sort of like that," Lauren snaps back.

And Lauren has but this is different. Erin is a genius of horrible. She can make it sound nice but this is just a really clever way to have a dig at me. I know I'm right because underneath people have commented with a whole load of crying with laughter emojis and **TRAGICS!** But there's no way to respond – if I have a go at her, it's ME who looks like a cow.

Lauren can see I'm flat, but she's acting all hard and odd. "Why don't you vlog about how falling over isn't the worst thing in the world, even though, at the moment, it feels like that. You do need to get over yourself a bit, Mills. It really could have been worse."

Lauren has completely failed to grasp that I'm having a total life disaster. All I can think of and all I can hear is the amount of people who are either laughing at me or feeling sorry for me all over the world.

"Bye, Millie. Hope you feel better."

You'd think your BFF would be able to MAKE you feel better. But Lauren just slinks off in the sunlight.

When I get back to Grandad's, I slam my bag on the sofa and sort of collapse like a massive splat of pasta sauce that's jumped off Teresa's plate. She's the world's messiest eater.

UNBELIEVABLY, Dad is home AND he actually notices that I am down. "What's up, Lady Mills?"

He says it like he thinks it's something minor. There's no point telling him about what Erin has done. He won't get it and will just say something sweet but useless. So I tell him that I fell over in the canteen and my chips went everywhere.

Dad doesn't laugh or say I'm being stupid. He looks at me and says, "You must have felt very embarrassed by that."

Which I did and I do, but, in a way, I want him to say, "Don't be silly, Millie! It's just a fall," or "Pick yourself up and get on with it!" like Mum would. But Dad is not Mum. He is sweet in a different way. In an understanding way. I can't believe I don't want understanding. What is happening to me?!

But now I've got Dad, I might as well talk to him.

"It's just that I remember you telling me about Nicholas Clarkson, Dad, and the time he lost his trunks – and that was twenty years ago. Even I can sing the song about him—"

Dad interrupts me. "Yes, I did tease him, Millie. But do you know what Nicholas Clarkson is doing now? He develops apps and software, drives a Porsche and goes to Barbados twice a year. I think he's got over the fact he was naked in a swimming pool decades ago. He probably swims naked out of choice in his own private swimming pool now. No one is laughing at him. He's laughing at us. Life is a marathon, Mills – not a sprint. And in the marathon, he's at the finish line getting his medal and bar of chocolate and I'm at Mile Two with a stitch in my side. I'm racing around trying to make money. I'm missing out on you growing up, even though you're here. I'm making a mess of it all, Millie…"

Dad looks gutted. The thing is, he's sort of right. He still lives with his dad and sister and I didn't see him for quite a long time.

But then I remember what Grandad told me. Dad's funny and kind. He's sweet to me. He still gets on with Mum.

"You're not making a mess of things. I think you're brilliant," I say and I give him a hug.

Dad has brought out my sensible, problem-sorter side again. I feel better.

"Oh, ignore your old dad. You make things excellent being here and I'm very proud of you. You won't end up like me. You, Millie, have BRAINS. Your dad's handsome looks –" and he winks – "but your mother's brain. If I were you, I would just forget about tripping over. It's a momentary lapse in a life that is otherwise fairly glorious, wouldn't you say?"

Dad pats me on the back and says, "Right, lady. What would you like for tea? Chips? CHIPS! CHIPS! Let's have chips, Millie. Let's re-establish chips as lovely things in your mind. LET US REHABILITATE THE MIGHTY CHIPO AND REMIND YOU THAT FRIED FOOD IS YOUR FRIEND!"

Dad shouting brings Grandad in. "What on earth is going on?" he grumbles. "Why are we shouting about chips? Is that what it's come to? Excitement about potatoes?"

Dad laughs and starts dancing round Grandad. "Yes! Yes! It has. Chips! Chips! FRIED BROWN CRISPY LOVELY CHHHHHHIPPPPPSSSSSS!"

"Daft fool!" Grandad eventually says. This makes both me and Dad giggle a lot.

I feel better and brave again.

"Can I borrow your shed, Grandad?"

"Well, I was going to escape from this house of nutters to do some potting but go on then. I can't be saved from them but perhaps you can."

Dad's chat has left me feeling a bit better. Why do these little things matter? They shouldn't. It's like everything gets completely blown out of proportion. And I want to tell everyone that they shouldn't and that you can lose your pants and still end up having amazing foreign holidays. I won't say that but I will tell people that TINY MISTAKES JUST DON'T MATTER. And Erin and her brilliant frayed-in-just-the-right-places jeans and her totally amazing way of being horrible, while pretending to be nice, can just go and CRASH in an "I've lost my Wi-Fi and nothing is downloading" way.

I don't want her to actually crash.

#KEEPINGiTREAL

I position the camera. I'm ready to share. I don't even message Lauren. She obviously doesn't care that much. I just do it.

"Hello. Millie Porter – back sooner than I thought. Thanks for all your comments. Well – thanks for the nice ones. The other ones – whatever.

"Today #Help Me Cope With Social Death. Those times when something horrible happens in front of everyone. Let me tell you what happened today. If you go to my school, you'll know already.

"Basically, I'd just collected my lunch from Mary the canteen lady and she has amazing dreads. Anyway, I was looking at her purple tips and pink roots and talking to my BFF Lauren and then, basically, I fell over my own feet and made a chip carpet. Which was embarrassing beyond belief. Can I just officially thank Lauren and the totally cool Gracie, who picked me up and didn't just stand there and stare or laugh or clap or whatever. Gracie – you have the best eye make-up ever and you are also actually a lovely person. Thank you. Also Bradley – thanks for the replacement food.

"Anyway. The aftermath of my fall is being shared around and that's pretty terrible. And you know what? I'm gutted but...

"No. I'm gutted.

"And I was going to hide away from it. But then I thought, "All I've done is drop some chips. SO TWONKING WHAT?! WHO CARES?!"

I start to get mad here.

"IT WAS SOME CHIPS ON A FLOOR. If a seagull had been in the school canteen, he would have been epically happy. I am SICK of feeling like my every move is being watched by people who cannot wait for me to go wrong. So this is ME, Millie, saying NOW – THESE PEOPLE LIKE MR STYLE SHAME WHO CALL PEOPLE OUT ON INSTAGRAM should be IGNORED. Stop looking at them. Falls are not that big a deal. NOR ARE LIFE FAILS AND FALLS. Really. And to prove that, I am going to fall over again."

(And I do. Badly. Spoon. But it makes my point.)

"No, there were no chips with that one but you get it.

"But I just want to say to you: if that happens to you, you don't need to hide away. You don't need to feel embarrassed or ashamed. You fell over. You dropped some chips. You did WHATEVER. You did not in any way hurt anyone. If you get caught doing something that makes you feel stupid, SO WHAT?! DROPPING YOUR LUNCH IS NORMAL. And you shouldn't have to feel bad about it.

"And another thing. Photos of people eating. No one looks glamorous when they are eating. I have here a sandwich made by my aunty Teresa. It has cheese and I am going to eat it.

"Do what you like. Do NOT BE SHAMED. This is Millie. #Help me to help you. Thank you. Goodnight - and don't feel bad about yourself!"

(And I take a massive bite of the sandwich and stop filming.)

Honestly, I don't feel very comfortable with how I look on-screen either. Even though I am real on my vlog, I'm not totally real. You can't share ALL of you. Like Grandad says, there'd be nothing left.

If I'm honest, it's not the same without Lauren. It's not as much fun and, without her, it's not as good. She's like my cheerleader.

I message her telling her I've uploaded a new video. I can see that she has read it but I get nothing back. What is wrong with her?! She sits on her phone. It's never out of her hand. It's—

MUM.

Oh, CHUFFING CHUFF.

She's shouting my name from outside. Why is she here? I must be in trouble again. There's no way she'd be round here at this time if I'm not.

#ANGRYMUM

Dad is hiding. He's stopped singing about chips because he can still read Mum's moods very well and she's not in a good one. He peeks out from behind the door in the hallway and pretends to cut his neck with his hand. This is our code for "She is ready to kill someone."

Aunty Teresa has decided the ice-cream van needs urgent maintenance (to be fair, it does and always will). Even Grandad has run to the shed. And he used to be a Royal Marine who lived on insect omelettes in the jungle and did twenty-mile runs with fourteen bricks in his rucksack. Or something.

Mum is terrifying. Magnificent but terrifying. Which is great when you're seven and your teacher makes you a tree in the Christmas play rather than a shepherd because she thinks "that's a job for boys". It's great when your mum storms up to the school to complain and the next thing you know, you're carrying a crook and Kyle Turner is being your sheep. That was fantastic but it's not so good now.

Mum does her quiet psycho voice. She doesn't lose her temper. She is reasonable. Apart from the time she threw a hand blender across the kitchen, she has always been a model of total control. Zero spoon and maximum excellence.

She stares at me.

"Millie, we need to talk. I'm worried you are giving away too much about your life online. Why do you want to share it all with strangers? Why can't you talk to me about all this? That's what I'm here for!"

"Mum!" I feel very like I know what I'm doing here. "I don't want to fall out with you about it but the whole point is my vlog is about being honest. I wanted to do something different and that means being REAL and—"

"Can I stop you there?" she interrupts. "Have you considered the implications of what you are doing? Look, Millie. I know you are very emotionally intelligent FOR YOUR AGE and always have been. I'm not going to patronize you. And I'm proud of you for trying to help people. But I'm your mother and it's my job to keep you safe and well. I've read the comments people have left and they are horrible. Horrible. And when I think of my little girl having to read that from ... well, I don't know what those people are but I don't want you anywhere near them, Millie. And don't tell me you're not affected by it because I know you are."

And I am affected. I really am. Who wouldn't be? It's awful.

Mum looks like she's about to sob massively. "You're my little girl."

This is my chance to explain. "Mum. You told me I should never stop what I want to do because other people laughed at me. You've always stuck up for me. That's why I became a shepherd and not a tree. Now I can fight trolls!"

"But you shouldn't have to!" Mum REALLY YELLS. "I nearly joined YouTube myself. I was going to call myself 'Millie's Mum' and have a go at all the tools that have said nasty things to you. You're very good, Millie. You present well and you're funny. And no, you don't need make-up. You can use it if you like to change your look but you don't need it. Come off YouTube, Millie. Please."

"I can handle it!" I yell.

"Can you really, Millie?" Mum whispers.

I look at Mum and start to cry. It just all hits me. The names. The "ugly" thing. The fountain of chips. Danny seeing me create a fountain of chips. Lauren being all cold and weird.

"See!" Mum hugs me. "This wouldn't have happened if you were still living with me."

"Oh Mum!" That just makes me cross. "Nothing would have happened if I still lived with you because I had to do everything your way. It wasn't all Gary and McWhirter's fault. It's you too! Even though I never did anything stupid, you always had to tell me what I should or shouldn't be doing."

This isn't fair AT ALL but I'm not feeling fair.

Mum sighs. "Perhaps I was a bit tough on you, but I'm so proud of what I've created. It's a tough world, Millie! VERY tough. Just give the vlogging a rest for a little while. That's the sensible thing to do."

I can't believe I'm saying this but I agree. "OK, I'll think about it."

Mum hugs me again and says, "Thank you."

She leaves and Dad comes out of hiding.

When I'm back in my bedroom I've got a message from Danny.

Sorry about the chips. The great news is, you
fall over really well. Can't wait to see how you
tackle exploding food in your vlog ☺

I don't think Danny is being horrible! He's trying to make me
smile. Like REAL friends do.

I message him.

I'm giving up #Help ☹

He responds immediately.

Why? Are you going to make a big announcement
about it?

The trolls and stuff… No. I haven't decided
what to do yet.

Millie, don't do this because of dumb comments.
You do know you're not ugly, don't you? Red-lipped
batfish – they are ugly. But not you.

What's a red-lipped batfish?

I'm almost frightened to ask.

It's this fish that looks like it's put red
lipstick on in the dark and has a lamp on its
head. It could never do a vlog. I saw it on Animal
Planet. Dad was building a naval destroyer and
there was nothing else on.

He sends me a photo of it.

I act cool. I don't know how to respond. So I don't. Why is
Danny telling me I'm not ugly? This feels weird.

My phone dings. Just when I thought my life couldn't get any
worse, I have a notification. Erin Breeler's new vlog has launched.
Of course I have to see it.

#KITTENS

Erin Breeler is wearing kitten ears. Even for a Monday, this is a new low.

She looks phenomenal on camera. The bedroom behind her has been lit perfectly. Her duvet is this Moroccan pattern with a matching lamp. Her dressing table is covered in cards and photos. It all looks so professional and perfect. She tilts her head in the classic Erin way and starts speaking.

"Hi! Do you like my ears? So, basically, a whole load of you have been saying, 'Erin, PLEASE do a vlog. Please.' And yeah. OK. OK with pleasure. And this is going to be about make-up and fashion and styling because ... that's what I do. I think when you come on here, you want to get away from all the awful stuff that's going on in your life. You don't want to be thinking about solving problems and how to deal with social embarrassment. This is all about looking good and feeling good and NOT—"

and she laughs this really annoying sweet but EVIL laugh –

"about how you recover from falling over..."

I turn it off.

I just don't want to watch any more

But I can't stop myself. I turn it back on.

Erin demonstrates different ways to wrap a scarf so it can be a sarong, a top, a headscarf and a skirt. She also shows how you can tie it to make a bag. THEN she gets a pair of thick tights and shares her secrets to the perfect rip.

It's an epic watch.

Erin's latest vlog is a fashion triumph.

My latest vlog is about dropping your lunch.

Already, she has had almost the same number of views as my cat vlog.

I think a break from vlogging is a very good idea indeed. I would also like a break from other people. Dave snuggles beside me. She may be wild but she understands a bad mood created by a good vlog better than any human ever could.

#WRAPPEDUP

Next day at school, Lauren isn't around. Maybe she's ill. It must be why she hasn't replied to my messages.

I'm on my own, so I try to do a Bradley and hug the walls. And I don't go anywhere near chips. I opt for a nice vegetarian wrap, as, even if you do drop them, the cheese, peppers and avocado are all contained. There won't be a food bomb. I'm just about to bite into it when someone sits beside me.

I assume it's lovely Gracie, so I say, "Wanna bite?"

A very Canadian voice answers, "Er … no, thank you – but thanks for asking."

I nearly choke. Danny Trudeau is sitting next to me.

"Ah, gone for the safe option today. The sturdy wrap. If it falls, it falls as ONE."

My mouth and brain sort of refuse to work together. I just stare.

Danny carries on. "I was thinking about what you said last night. I like #Help and I don't want you to stop vlogging. It's … interesting. It's something new and it's different. I get kinda bored with all the make-up stuff or the wacky prankster vloggers. I think it's great you're so real."

(This is just what Bradley said – he was RIGHT!)

"It's sweet to want to help people out. It's a hard world. It's nice to watch something that makes you laugh – especially after moving here and not knowing anyone. You know I think the dinosaurs died out because they had no TV and died of boredom."

"Really?" This is the only word I manage to say. I must look really confused.

"Yeah." Danny smiles. "Just think, at the end of a hard day chasing stuff, you just want to get back to your cave and watch something."

At first I don't laugh because I don't really get it. Then I remember – that vlog where I said that dinosaurs died out about because they didn't embrace feminism…

"Oh. Yeah." I'm in a panic. "They did need TV. They needed a show featuring a really glamorous family of brontosauruses. They could call it *Keeping up with the Jurassics* or something."

This isn't meant to be a brilliantly hilarious joke but Danny tilts his head back and howls like a maniac. He laughs so loudly that basically everyone who wasn't looking is now looking.

Including Erin. She's staring at us HARD.

Oh, please don't talk to me when she's looking.

"Anyway," Danny interrupts my head panic. "I just wanted to tell you that. It's neat. You're neat. And I like what you said about falling over not being the end of the world. It's not. It's just falling over. Life is falling over, you know, and getting back up again."

So he's not just good-looking, he's sensible too. And a philosopher. I clearly want to snog him immediately. Like now. But instead, I say, "Thanks, Danny. That's … good."

I can't really concentrate because now BRADLEY is walking up to my table looking really grumpy.

Danny quickly leaves and Bradley sits down. "Are you two going out?"

"No!" I sort of half yell and half whisper. "He just wanted to tell me I was … neat."

"Good!" Bradley snaps. I stare at him.

Bradley sees me looking at him in a strange way. "Well, I don't think you'd enjoy going out with a Canadian. He'll probably fly back there soon and I know from my lift contacts that Canadians are very … different. They probably hide behind all those maple leaves and do their dating in forests."

I think this is Bradley trying to be funny. It's not really.

"Bradley, he was only being nice. He's interested in the vlog. Right, I've just got to go and ask Gracie where she gets her mascara from. It wouldn't run in a monsoon. It's EPIC!"

I know any make-up talk will send Bradley away nicely. And it does.

I leave the canteen. As I turn the corner to the main block of the school, my path is blocked. What blocks me is solid, tall and very scary. Glossy lips shine like very dangerous Olympic ski slopes. Teeth as white as gourmet ice cream frozen with liquid nitrogen gleam at me.

It's Erin.

"Millie Porter," she says. "It's time you and me had a talk."

#SHOWDOWN

Erin does her beautiful head tilt and snarls. She's whispering, but to me her message is loud and clear.

"You think you're cool. You're not."

I go all pathetic. "I don't think I'm cool at all."

"Yes, you do," she whispers. "But YOU are small. My vlog has already had thousands of views. No one wants to see you giving us your advice. Who do you think you are?"

This makes me angry and I have an attack of the braves.

"I've had loads of views too. And I know you've looked at my vlogs because of your Instagram. And I think you've been doing some enormous trolling."

Erin tilts her head to the other equally glamorous side. We should ALL be over girl-on-girl hate but Erin makes it impossible.

"The trolling is nothing to do with me," she growls. "I don't mind telling you what I think of you to your face. Do you know what people say about you behind your back? That you're DULLSVILLE! That you're a spoon. That you think not wearing make-up is a new thing that makes you some kind of amazing rebel.

You're not going to change the world and get a prize, Millie. It's all been done. And people are doing it BETTER."

I start to lose it now. "I KNOW. All I'm trying to do is help people because I'm dull and sensible, Erin! And because being around you has totally taught me how to deal with twonks who only love themselves and want to make other people's lives a misery."

And then Erin goes all Disney evil queen and says, "I can destroy you. Never forget it. Leave this to the people who actually know what they're doing and have something to say. Leave Instagramming to people who want to make this world look better, not worse. Basically, Millie BORING Porter – WIND IT IN, DO ONE and DISAPPEAR!"

She still isn't finished though.

"Oh, and don't for one second think that Danny is interested in you. We're going bowling after school this week. That was a pity chat. He's a nice boy and he feels SORRY for you. Not attracted to you. Boys like him would never go out with girls like you. This isn't cute fairy-tale land where the gorgeous boy likes the clever girl. Go and have your happy ending with the lift geek. You can spend your time pressing buttons and misusing the emergency bell. Thrilling!"

Then Erin Breeler glides off.

My mind tries to find lots of amazing things to say. I reach right into my brain but I've got nothing. So I stand there like the goldfish Dave brought in from someone's pond once. All tragic and flapping and gasping for air. Erin has played with me like Dave played with that fish and now she's dumped me in the kitchen by the microwave, expecting someone else to clean me up.

I'm destroyed.

I'm having a full-on attack.

I need to get away NOW.

#ESCAPE

I rush to the Zen loo. My heart is pumping like it would if I'd been in a situation of extreme terror. I've googled this. It's very unlikely I will die from this Erin attack – it just feels like it at the moment. I splash water on my face and breathe in deep breaths. And then I go into a cubicle and cry and cry till my face probably looks like a red-lipped batfish.

WHERE IS LAUREN WHEN I NEED HER?! Trust her to have the flu when I'm having a minor meltdown.

When I leave, Bradley is waiting for me AGAIN. "Do you need more toilet roll, Millie?"

"No, I'm OK," I sniff. "How did you know I was here?"

"I guessed," Bradley whispers. "The whole school is talking about it. There's a photo of you and Erin. It was a Snapchat but it's been screengrabbed. I think she probably had someone waiting to take it. It was a planned attack. An ambush."

"Is it bad?" I don't really want to know the answer.

"No, it just looks like you're talking."

"We weren't. She went for me."

"Of course she did, Millie! You are totally being successful just being you and you're getting attention. Sometimes, getting bombed is a sign of success!"

I sniff. I can't stop crying.

"I think I'm the stupidest person in the world. I don't feel wise any more."

Bradley smiles at me and gives me a big hug. It's surprisingly nice being hugged by Bradley. "No, you're not stupid. I've had my trousers on inside out for two hours today. Everyone knows my mum shops at Tesco now and that I am size aged fifteen."

This makes me smile a bit. It reminds me of the sort of thing Lauren would say. Lozza is a queen. And she's sweet and funny and kind and her occasional toolness only hurts her. Never anyone else. Except that time with the squirrel. And we don't talk about that.

Why hasn't she messaged me? I MISS HER.

"Come on, Millie," Bradley says. "Don't let her see that she has made you feel bad."

I look at him. "What I really need now is some cucumber. Not to scare cats with – to put on my eyes to reduce inflammation. Or teabags. They tend to be more common than cucumbers in schools and life generally."

And then something comes over me. Rushing and real. Confused but certain at the same crashing time. I kiss Bradley Sanderson hard on the lips. And just as he puts his arm round me, I pull back.

Bradley has gone bright red but looks quite pleased.

"OR," I quickly continue, "I should wear my enormously glam and exceedingly slightly ludicrous sunglasses ALL day. That will make me look like I'm hiding after a scandal, though."

Bradley pauses. "Well, um – you are really, Millie."

Bradley is right. This is what everyone will be talking about for months. The day that Erin took down Millie Porter. It will become legend. I bet Erin is already planning the statue that will go on the spot. I will for ever be cast in bronze as…

OK, my head is probably going a bit crazy there. But still. This is big. And why did I kiss Bradley Sanderson?

#TWISTED

"You can't be beaten by her!"

At the end of school, I call Aunty Teresa and tell her everything – apart from Bradley.

"Do you want me to have a word with her, Mills?"

I have a vision of Aunty Teresa turning up to school in her ice-cream van and shoving a giant cone in Erin's FACE. It's a lovely fantasy that I may think about for days.

Gracie comes up to me mid Aunty Teresa's anti-Erin ranting and makes a motion that I need to get off the phone FAST.

"Millie. I don't know how to break this to you and PLEASE DON'T TELL ANYONE I TOLD YOU but … Erin is telling everyone that you were having a go at her. The Snapchat shows you and her arguing. The fact is, you look very cross. You look like the one who is laying into her and telling her to back off. Have a look!"

Sure enough, when I see them, what I thought was my blank look of spoon actually seems like a death stare. Bradley was COMPLETELY wrong when he said it looked like we were just talking. I'm like a cheetah eyeing up a gazelle before getting it by the neck, ripping it to pieces and then eating it in front of a really excited cameraman.

"It does look a bit … bad."

I can't believe how she can twist things.

"What can I do about it?"

Gracie goes very quiet and then says, "Nothing, Millie. You can't fight that. You can't beat her. She's amazing." Gracie realizes what she's said. "Horrible, don't get me wrong, but amazing."

I look over to the edge of the mobile classrooms that were meant to be temporary but have been there since Roman times and see a crowd of girls comforting Erin. She shakes her head and looks upset but when she catches me looking at her, she flashes a perfect grin. There are already sharks with cameras walking round menacing people. I've seen them. They are called Erin. That's what I would have to tell Bradley. If I hadn't kissed him.

#REVENGE

At home, things seem a bit better. Teresa and Dad are doing a dance routine to an old song called "Groove Is in the Heart". Grandad is tutting and shaking his head but looking impressed at the same time.

Dave is sleeping on top of a perfectly ironed pile of washing. She's moulting and she's created a new teensy, tabby hair jumper on top of a pair of Grandad's cords. He'll go mad when he sees them, so I take Dave to the back garden for a brush. Dave purrs and rolls with pleasure, then bites me when she's had enough. If humans treated hairdressers this way, they'd be sent to prison.

When I get back inside, there's a message from Gracie.

Millie. Don't get freaked out again.

(This means there's totally something to get freaked out about.)

But have a look at Erin's Instagram.

My heart goes into my mouth. When I look, there's a beautiful black and white photo of Erin looking sad. What is it about black and white? It could make anything look arty and serious. Even Dave the girl cat thug would look arty with that filter. Erin has hashtagged it #sad #leaving #unhappy and written:

So, anyway, I've been really struggling with some of the things that have been said to me on here and in person. Someone attacked me today and said that I should leave all this to the people who do it better. Look at me. It hurt. IT HURTS.

I am going to come off social media for a time. I think that way I can just get my head together. And that means my vlog too. I only ever started it as a bit of fun and I do not deserve the abuse I am getting from certain people. Plus, I have to tell you I need to concentrate on my personal life a bit more. I know lots of you are going to be very disappointed by this but the truth is, everyone has their limits and I have reached mine. Love you. Erin x

I cannot believe people are falling for Erin's total "I am a victim" nonsense. All the things SHE said to me she's now saying that I said. I didn't. I wouldn't. That's just not me. I wish it was. But it's NOT.

The comments that have already been left are unbelievable.

Don't let the haters get you down.

Name and shame the bullies here. I will personally go after them.

After my dog died, your Instagram page was the one thing that made me smile again. You bring joy to millions. Don't stop.

That is totally her making up her own comments.

I ring Lauren. There's still no answer.

I can't believe Erin is making me out to be completely evil and horrible when SHE is the one who is causing all the problems! SHE's having a go at me and now she is making out that she is the victim. Some people might actually believe that I'm like that and YES, by "some people" I do mean Danny.

Danny.

Danny would want me to do a vlog now. Wouldn't he?

So would Bradley.

I'm going to do a vlog. It doesn't have to be aimed at Erin. It can just be about how people can say what they like about you on social media and that you have absolutely no control over it.

I've got to say something.

#CATASTROPHE

In Grandad's shed, it's just me and Dave. Everyone in the house is either dancing or pretending not to enjoy dancing, so this is the best place to be.

I don't feel like vlogging but I do.

"Hello. Millie here and I'm feeling a bit rubbish."

(At this point, Dave jumps on my lap. I think she feels bad about biting me after I'd made her look good.)

"#Help Me Cope When People Say Things Which Are Clearly NOT TRUE.

"So Dave and me are just sitting here and I've been wondering what you think about what I'm doing on here. The thing is, I can't bear the thought of anyone hating me. I make out that I don't care but I do. And it's the hardest thing because I really do want people to like me. God, that sounds PATHETIC. But I do."

(I look at Dave. It's random but I have an idea.)

"This is Dave my cat. She's a girl but she's called Dave. You might have seen her in some of my other vlogs. Anyway, Dave doesn't really care about anyone or what they think. She does what she likes. And yes – she's a cat but there's a lot to be

196

learnt from her attitude. I know people who HATE Dave and think she's a walking fur menace, er … a bag of fleas, a pit bull in a cat body – people say all sorts of things about her and she just carries on doing her thing.

"And that's kind of what I want to say. I get people asking me about what to do when people say horrible or untrue things on the Internet. And something happened to me this week where someone was basically making me out to be a Queen of Evil when actually they were the person who was … just being nasty and oh … hugely a SPOON. And some people believe it because they want to believe it. There's nothing I can do about it. I just have to know that the people who matter know what I'm really like.

"The thing is, it still hurts. It REALLY DOES, but I look at Dave and I think about that time that my mum's next-door neighbour called her the worst cat on earth and accused her of getting her pedigree cat pregnant till she found out Dave was actually a girl and not a lesbian either. Dave just took the abuse and carried on using their cat flap to steal food. We've all just got to keep on being ourselves and ignoring the haters and, as I always say, please tell someone. I know. I KNOW! Boring advice. Dullsville Central but seriously Johnny Mint and the Minters is the result you'll get if you just talk to people you love and trust and um … yep. That's it from me. Be more like Dave."

And at that point, Dave attacks the phone because she feels like it. So I add:

"But don't attack phones or sit on freshly washed trousers and shed your hair. Also, if you wake me up at 5 a.m. by punching my face because you want food, you won't be popular.

"Thanks again. Millie over and out. #Help me to help you - although today, I think I need help more than anyone."

This says everything I want it to even though it suggests humans should be more like scabby, slightly insane cats.

I'm uploading it though. At least it's me doing something.

I give Dave a special hug. She may be full of fleas but she really is an icon for modern women. And cats. And probably even dogs if they would just listen.

#BFFRESCUE

The next day, Lauren is off sick. AGAIN. She normally likes Wednesdays too. And as I'm also avoiding both Danny and Bradley, the day goes really slowly. I get to check the comments on my vlog once. They are mainly about Dave.

Dave though.

Cat BAE

Both need thereapy... (Spell *therapy* right if you are going to suggest it!)

Nothing wrong with lesbian cats. Love is love.

I feel like replying, "I am totally for marriage equality." Then I realize cats can't get married anyway. Or perhaps they do and just don't invite us.

When I get home, I find Aunty Teresa is dressed in Victorian clothes and talking to herself.

"And they say that if you come here at night, you will see the ghost of a man who drowned after tending an injured duck. Close your eyes tightly and you will hear his gentle quacking— Oh, hello, Millie!" she says when she spots me. "I'm just practising! Me and your dad are doing a ghost walk."

"I didn't know there were any ghosts round here." I'm used to being confused by Teresa but this is totally bizarre.

"Oh, there's not!" Aunty Teresa says casually. "We're just going to make them up."

"You can't do that!" I shout. "It must be illegal!"

"Yes we can, Millie. Someone made it all up once. Why not us? We will live in legend. WE WILL CREATE LEGEND!" Teresa roars.

Dad thunders into the room dressed as a ghost. He asks Teresa, "Is this going to work?"

I answer for her. "No, Dad – it's not. You don't look like a ghost. You look like a sheet."

"Actually, clever clogs," Dad says, "I'm a Roman. This is a toga. I'm the ghost of Emperor Caesar!"

This is too much. "Dad! Emperor Caesar never lived round here. That's just a load of—"

Teresa gets quite aggressive. "You cannot prove, Millie, that Caesar did not come here on holiday. And anyway, there were lots of Caesars."

"There was only one Caesar round here," I say, "and he was actually a salad."

When Teresa and Dad are like this, there's only one place to go – away.

I sit in my room and think about Lauren. This is the longest we've gone without speaking. And she wasn't even off school this long when she had conjunctivitis. I check all her accounts. She's posted a rainbow meme on Instagram with some ridiculous quote about *There can be no rainbow without a storm.*

So she can't look after me in my hour of total need but she's well enough to make other people happy. I feel a bit … rejected.

I check my views. There are a few more but no new subscribers. And all the new comments are about Dave.

Gonna change my name to Dave. TRIBUTE.

More Le Chat. Less Chat.

I hate it when people try to be clever and funny and they're NEITHER. It's just annoying.

Dear Brain – think about something that makes you feel good. NOT Bradley. Think about Danny. Please don't let Erin's post have made him think I'm a cow.

I catch up on Canada. Basically, we have the same Queen but they have better ice cream and it's bigger. Also, there are more things that can kill you in Canada, like snakes, spiders and the West Nile virus which basically makes your brain explode. And if that doesn't get you, then the bears will and the only way to stop them attacking is to pretend you are dead already and hope it's a stupid one.

I take a deep breath. I imagine what would happen if me and Danny ever became a "thing". I'd probably say we should live here. I can't do bears. Or elks. They charge during the mating season. I don't even want to watch things with antlers kissing. *Don't charge at me for accidentally stumbling on your love thing like a spoon. I didn't mean to. It was an accident! Carry on kissing your moosey girlfriend.*

Why am I talking to an imaginary elk?

You know why. Love sends you crazy.

Teresa walks into my bedroom. "Sorry. Don't mind me," she tries to whisper. "We just need more paranormal props for the ghost walk. Does this Barbie look spooky to you?"

I look at her. "She's got one arm, so I suppose so."

"Yeah," Aunty Teresa agrees. "I'm going to say it was the voodoo doll used in a ritualistic murder that happened in this house."

"There WILL be a murder here in a minute if someone doesn't come and tidy up this front room!" Grandad yells from the bottom of the stairs.

"Be honest, Mills. What's more disturbing – a one-armed Barbie or a Furby with a pulled-out eye?"

"Why don't you use them both?" I suggest. "You could call them a Duo of Death."

"Millie!" Aunty Teresa rushes over and hugs me. "Every so often, I sense you have a spark of our entrepreneurial spirit, our *joie de vivre*, our—"

Now Grandad bursts in. Why is there no privacy in this house?

"You're being ruddy crackers. Don't get involved, Millie. Never mind ghosts, these two will put me in an early grave."

Grandad looks at me. "And will you be requiring my shed today for one of your things that you do for your friends on the phone?"

I look at Grandad and say, "No," without letting my face say, "I AM HIDING AWAY FROM THE ENTIRE WORLD."

Grandad just shuffles off. Sometimes, I am tremendous at pretending things are OK when they are quite clearly NOT.

Five minutes later, when I am still feeling quite excellent about fooling Grandad, Mum texts me. She still texts – even though it costs money. She says she "doesn't trust the other things".

Anything you'd like to tell me, Millie?

I reply.

No. Why? Love you x

She replies instantly.

No reason. No problem. I'm here if you need me.
Love you XX

I think Mum has a mind-melding machine in her head and she knows everything that goes on in my brain. Which is a worry. For both of us.

Just realized mind melds are what they do in *Star Trek*. Sometimes, it scares me how deep Bradley has got into my head. He's there all the time like a small glowing lift, going up and down the floors of my brain. Never stopping. Just up and down. Waiting for me to get on and get in touch with him.

Which I still haven't done since I kissed him.

And then I realize that makes me sound like the most full-of-myself, love-yourself spoon since Erin Breeler and her elephant ego, so I stop.

I'm making this into something it's not. I'm sure he thinks that kiss was as weird as I did. Bradley loves the fact that I quite admire escalators. Not me. If he liked me, he would have totally made a move after I kissed him but he hasn't.

Erin. I wonder if she's seen my vlog. I check Instagram. Sure enough, she's at the top of my feed.

Her latest photo is a STUNNING one of her and her friends. They are angled and contoured immaculately. Erin's cheekbones look like they've been created from a really lovely bit of marble kitchen work surface. Pale and perfect with a flash of pink. She looks unbelievable. It must have taken about five attempts to get it just right but it was clearly worth it. Underneath, she's written:

I'm BACK! I decided that you can't let the haters win and today, I had such a wonderful day. After school, me and some BFFs went shopping (YES! I have more than one BFF!) and all the love was there. I will share what we bought later. (I think you will LOVE it – but don't get too excited. Just one jacket but a WONDERFUL one.) I want to thank you ALL so, so much for your support during this tough time. I came back from my break to find so many beautiful messages from all over the world encouraging me to carry on sharing. And I'm going to. You have made me feel like a total superstar. Thank you SO MUCH. I will never again let the jealousy of some people stop what I'm doing or who I talk to. I LOVE YOU x

YET AGAIN, there is nothing there that I can moan about. But, underneath it all I know the message is "BACK OFF, MILLIE. I have the power. I have the masses on my side. If you attack, I will find not just one but a hundred ways to hurt you."

Right now, I'm the stranded whale of the social media world. Everyone will come to look at me on the beach as I struggle desperately to get oxygen. Some will feel very sorry for me. But they won't be able to get me back to the sea. And all the time, Erin will be stood by a sand dune taking selfies with me flapping in the background.

I'm getting myself into a right state about everything.

I pick up the phone and call Lauren. FINALLY, she answers! I tell her what has happened but she doesn't seem to listen. There's lots of "yeahs" and "mmmms", which are totally unhelpful. She almost seems in a bit of a diva strop – very unlike Lauren.

"The thing is," I say to her, "I need to do SOMETHING!"

"No, you don't," Lauren snaps. Now I'm really worried. She doesn't get how serious all this is.

"Lauren! All my subscribers will be looking to me for a way to respond to her!"

"No, they won't, Millie. You can do a one-minute-long vlog: 'What to do when you're caught out. Well, you just have to take it on the chin and move on. Thanks. Bye.' That's what you should do."

Lauren sounds angry. Almost … nasty.

"You think it's as simple as that?"

"Probably, Millie. Anyway, stuff is going on here, so I've got to go. Bye."

I say, "OK. Bye!"

But inside I'm broken and absolutely gutted. And what stuff is going on that Lauren can't speak to me about?! That's total spoon behaviour from her.

Or…

Or perhaps she's been kidnapped and she's being held hostage and can't talk to me.

Perhaps "stuff" is a code word for really bad stuff involving mad extremists who want to make the country YouTube-free or Lauren-free or something.

Or perhaps she's cross with me. Though I can't think why. I've told her everything that's happened with the vlog while she's been away.

Either way, I can't sit here and let my friend become a statistic or fall out with me. I need to go over to her house to find out what's going on. I wonder whether I should take back-up but in a house full of ghosts and old people, it's better, as Grandad says, to be a lone soldier of fortune. With a phone. I take that obviously. You can't be without your phone. That would be insane.

#BFFGONEBAD

This is scary, and mid-week should not be about face-to-face combat. It's a drastic measure but some things need sorting right now. As I go round the corner to Lauren's house, I start to case out the joint. I watched this on a private investigator's vlog once. You assess the hostility and the threat.

Lauren's dad is mowing the lawn, so I decide that perhaps I may have overreacted – but I was right to check. You can't be too careful.

Lauren's dad can't hear me over the hum of the mower. It's odd because the grass doesn't look like it needs cutting, but you can't argue with gardeners. I know that from Grandad.

I run upstairs to see Lauren. She's sitting on her bed and barely looks at me. "Oh, you've remembered I exist?"

"Lauren! What is UP with you? Why haven't you replied to any of my messages or been at school? Are you ill? You've been acting like a TOTAL cow."

She gives me a look she's never given me before. She looks like she's about to explode. Then she sneers, "I'm surprised you've noticed. You're so in love with those people on your vlog. Or Danny. Or Bradley."

OH. So she isn't in any danger from a terrorist group. She's actually just JEALOUS. This makes me LIVID.

"Well, Lauren, sorry to tell you this but people on there actually need me. They look to me for a bit of good sense and stuff. A bit of—"

Lauren gets off her bed and starts screaming. Actual, total RAGE. "I need you and I'm actually real! I helped you make that vlog WHAT IT IS! Have you noticed that I'm having the worst time at home ever?! My parents are at war. I don't even know where my mum is right now. My dad isn't speaking to anyone and is mowing dirt. HE IS TRYING TO MOW ACTUAL MUD. I am going through HELL. And all you care about these days is your views. Your views?! Who do you think you are?! WHY DO YOU EVEN BOTHER?! You've been totally taken in by it all, Millie. Everything you say and do is about your YouTube channel and your friends on there. And I was happy to help but now it's taken over. You don't need my advice. Go and speak to one of your many friends –" Lauren keeps making little speech marks every time she says the word *friends* – "YOU don't need a best friend. You need a public relations manager!"

This makes me cross. I've totally been there for Lauren. All the time. OK, I might have got a bit distracted lately. But she obviously can't deal with the fact that I have different friends and different interests and – YES! – I have done something that a lot of – well, some – people are getting comfort from. Perhaps I haven't asked her about stuff as much as I should have but I'm so cross at her for ruining it all I end up yelling, "Your parents have been rubbish for years. What's new?!"

Even as I'm saying these words, I know they sound totally awful. Enormous levels of awful too. But I can't stop.

Lauren goes a funny colour. "You know what, Millie? You're right. Yes, they have been. And you've been really great about it. You've really helped me. But recently, it's just been all about you. Or you and Erin. Who cares what she thinks? And also, the way you've been treating Bradley is just—"

"Just WHAT?" And this I really want to know because it will totally prove that Lauren is being completely HORRIBLE and really, she's just upset at her mum and dad. That's fine but be angry at them! Don't have a go at me!

"You KNOW Bradley likes you!" Lauren shouts. "You KNOW he does! But you keep on pretending that he doesn't and hanging out with him so he'll help you with your vlog. And if Mr Sexy Maple Leaf wasn't already dating Erin Breeler, you wouldn't even talk to Bradley! That's not fair!"

I'm not having this.

"Lauren. We. Are. Friends. Are you saying women can't be friends with men? I'm sorry, Lauren, but that is totally unfeminist. Bradley is responsible for his emotions – not me!"

(I saw that phrase in an article online – it sounds good.) I'm also trying really hard not to think about the fact I've snogged him and not told my best friend.

"It's got nothing to do with feminism, Millie! It's got everything to do with not being a cow. You always bring up the clever stuff when you want to win a row or look cool. How about just not being a spoon that only cares about herself and her PROFILE! I know I'm not the only person who has parents that have split up. I know that. But today, I'm the only ex-best friend of yours that has. I'm the only person I know who woke up to her mum crying and packing a suitcase and saying "Sorry" to me repeatedly. My mum left home today! Left my DAD and left HOME! But, don't worry, I understand that, to you, YouTube is more important."

Now I feel DREADFUL.

"It's not!" I whisper. "I'm not a mind-reader! Why didn't you tell me?"

"I couldn't get a word in!" Lauren says through tears. "And you haven't asked me what's going on in my life for ages. I'm sorry Erin isn't very nice to you, but so? You were the one she got today. There'll be another one tomorrow. And the next day. That's what Erin does. You can't change it."

I start to think. "Do you really think I've treated Bradley badly?"

Lauren throws her hands in the air. "Oh, we're back to YOU again! Do me a favour, Millie. Just GO! GO! You're not a person I like right now. You've been completely messed up by a tiny bit of fame. HASHTAG DREADFUL USELESS COMPLETELY POINTLESS BEST FRIEND."

I start to cry. Lauren starts to cry.

As I leave, I notice that Lauren's dad has been mowing the same bit of mud during the entire time I've been with her. He didn't see me arrive and he doesn't see me leave. I think Lauren could get kidnapped and he wouldn't notice. Perhaps I wouldn't notice either. I'd be too busy uploading or recording or something.

I'm useless.

Hashtag dreadful useless completely pointless best friend. I never thought that would be aimed at me. But it might be true. It IS true. Very true.

#ESCALATION

Yes. All this has escalated quickly. Not in a Bradley way. In a bad-without-any-amazing-moving-stairs way...

Back in my bedroom, life seems completely grim. I'm a bad daughter to my mum, a useless friend, I hurt lovely men, I'm a bad feminist or a good one that's bad (I can't decide which) and I've forgotten my cat needs her one-drop flea treatment and currently she's scratching in a way that says she needs it.

How do I even have the nerve to do an advice vlog?! My life is a total and utter mess. I want to ring my mum but that will just remind me that I don't get on with her either. Her answer to everything is to tell me to come home. I can't go back there. I can't go back to that level of clean.

Perhaps I'm a grot too.

The fact is, I've failed at just about everything. I've upset everyone who has ever been lovely to me ... and now I'm looking at Aunty Teresa, who's standing at the end of my bed dressed as Queen Victoria. She has frills, bum and tum pillow padding and everything.

"Hello, Mills. Me and your dad have had this idea that we want to put to you... We want you to come and join us. Be part of what will become the biggest ghost tour in the country. We want you to do ALL our social media. We thought we could get you to pretend on your advice vlog that you had someone write to you about seeing a ghost. THEN you get me on to talk about what you do when you have a ghost in your house and THEN, at the end, you say, 'Thank you, Teresa – poltergeist specialist who organizes the ghost tour every Thursday and Tuesday from 6 p.m., concessions available, and if you book as a group, a can of Coke is included in your entrance fee.' It's not proper Coca-Cola, it's the cheap supermarket stuff – but we don't have to mention that, do we? I don't think so."

Aunty Teresa doesn't realize I've been crying, so I just say, "I don't think I'll be doing my vlog for a bit."

"OK," she says, "but there's something else. You see, for the ghost tour, we need a younger female actor to play a little Victorian match girl who dies horribly from being really cold without a decent duffel coat."

"It's called hypothermia," I say.

"Yeah. That!" Teresa says. "So you basically have to just stand there and say stuff like, 'I'm freezing' and 'Would you like to buy some matches? It doesn't matter if you don't smoke. You can use them to light your scented candles.' What do you think?"

"I don't think they had scented candles in Victorian times." Even for Teresa, this sounds crazy.

"Whatever!" she says excitedly. "You can freestyle. Shiver a bit. You can moan too. It'll be really –" and Teresa pulls this super serious face and twiddles her fingers – "eerie."

Usually, I'd be shouting, "NO WAY!" but my mouth hurdles over my brain and says yes. Perhaps it's about time I did something for someone else. I want to take my mind off everything. Ghosts will do that. And let's be honest – I've reached peak dork on the vlog. What could possibly be worse than that?

"Just promise there'll be no photos shared on the Internet. ANYWHERE."

Teresa slightly looks away from me. "I can't promise that completely, as anyone can be snapped these days, but I will tell people not to take photos of the match girl because it's dangerous while our workers are channelling spirits."

"Just to be clear, Teresa," I say, "I'm not pretending to channel anything. I'm only doing this as a favour."

"I know." Teresa hugs me very tightly. "And I really appreciate it."

That's not completely the truth though. Doing something, ANYTHING, will take my mind off things. Even if that anything is pretending to be a starving under-age worker in a vintage dress.

"Oh," Teresa adds quickly, "by the way, we start tomorrow night. Hope that's OK for you. Here's your tray. All you have to do is tie the ribbons around your neck and pretend to be ill. Try some flour on your face. That trick regularly got me off school, I looked so ill. I'll leave your costume out for you. See you at six outside the old church that's been converted into a posh block of flats – you know the one – opposite the driving-test centre."

Teresa disappears very quickly.

I may die a social death but not an actual death. Being a starving Victorian match girl will hopefully remind me that life isn't so bad, even though, at the moment, it feels terrible.

I'm having a sensible burst again. I'm still in there somewhere!

#GHOSTBUSTERS

For most of Thursday, I opt for a social coma at school. I'm physically present but not mentally there. Lauren is still away and I have enough hiding spots to avoid all boys. I spend all of lunch in the Zen loo. Lovely Gracie was worried I was in there too long. I told her I'd been having a nap.

I was glad to get home, until I saw what I had to wear for the ghost tour.

There are no two ways about it. I'm dressed up in an old lace nightie and cardigan, with batter mix on my face. I look like the ghost of a pancake. Not of a little match girl. Also I'm very, very cold. So I may be dying an actual death too. Teresa has made sure I'm on a main road. This is great for personal safety but not great for how many people are staring at me. I wish she would hurry up.

Just as I'm seriously thinking of packing everything in and going home, I hear Teresa and the group of ghost hunters coming towards us. She's telling them that the church couldn't be turned into flats until they'd rid the place of the ghost of a sad, weeping match girl who died of cold in the graveyard.

I stiffen up, knowing this is my cue to start moaning and acting generally very ill indeed.

Teresa turns the corner and says, "Behold the little match girl! See her terrible rags. We will tell the horrible story about how no one would buy her matches and how she died because of the cruelty of Victorian society. And how she's back, haunting these posh flats because she wants to remind the rich people of today that having really nice Ikea lampshades and probably underfloor heating isn't enough. You need to be a NICE PERSON too."

I know for a fact that Teresa is saying this because she is jealous that she couldn't afford one of the posh flats.

At this point, I say in a really feeble voice, "Buy a match from a poor match girl. Buy a match…"

As I slump like a really ill person, I notice a figure towards the back of the ghost-hunter crowd. Staring at me and flashing me a smile that would probably bring a very dead person back to life is Danny. And two people that look a lot like they could be his parents.

And Erin.

And I'm dressed as a match girl with food smeared all over my face.

I've probably had worse days in my life but I can't remember one.

I wave at Danny. He bounds over to me, leaving Erin with his parents.

"Hello," I whisper and pull a "this is actually really embarrassing" face.

Teresa growls at me, "Ghosts don't wave at their earthly friends!"

But just as Teresa tries to shoo Danny away, a man in a suit races out from the posh flats and starts yelling, "Oi! YOU! Get lost. Spreading rumours about this place could take ten grand off my property price! Move yourself!"

Aunty Teresa shouts, "This is a public right of way and I can tell people what I like!"

Someone in the crowd yells, "Is this not true then?"

"Of course it's not true!" the man in the suit says. "She's making money off of gormless tourists like you!"

Teresa goes quiet and then says, "You can't prove that!"

At this point, all the crowd starts tutting and heading their separate ways. Teresa says, "No … no! Look! Look at the match girl! She'll die without your fee."

Just about everyone rolls their eyes at Teresa.

"Why didn't you take the money at the start?!" I ask her.

Teresa is furious. "I didn't think my match girl would start chatting up the punters!"

I'm adding Teresa to the "Doesn't like Millie much at the moment" list.

Danny, who has hung around, ignores the fact I have gone bright red under my pancake mix. "Can I buy some matches please?" Then he winks.

"What are you doing here?" I ask him.

"I like to find out about social history. I like to know the facts about different places."

"Me too," I say. "For example, I totally know what to do when a randy elk charges at you after you've stared at his girlfriend."

"What's that?" Danny says.

"Run!"

I think at this point I am both wise and slightly hilarious.

However, I can see that Danny is wondering why I've started going on about elks.

Why have I started going on about elks?

"Anyway," he says, "we're, er, going for a pizza with my parents. Want to come too?"

It's the right thing to do but it's obvious he doesn't want me to come. Erin and me. It's just not going to work.

"Er … no. I'd better get home and check that my aunty is OK." I also think eating a margherita dressed as a Victorian match girl may not be a good look.

"OK," Danny says, sort of gratefully. "Catch you another time."

"Yes!" I say and I wave goodbye to him and Erin. Erin doesn't wave back. She's too busy taking photos.

Goodbye, perfect man. Matches, elks and the fact I'm a useless person have come between us but that is just today. The worst day in history. This is like the last day in Pompeii when Vesuvius exploded. I am currently breathing in hot volcanic rock of embarrassment and I'm dying. My fossilized remains will be discovered in 2,000 years from now and people will know that I died of terminal spoon.

I just need to get home and talk to someone.

#OVERANDOUT

By the time I get home I'm just about over everything and I don't care. I wipe the batter off my face, get changed out of my costume and go to the shed. Dave follows me in. She's still scratching and disappears behind me to tackle her fleas in peace.

I've learnt a lot these last few days. I feel I could share something REALLY useful. And who cares about subscribers or trolls or any of it. This could save someone from what I've suffered. It's time for a really REAL vlog. I turn on the camera.

"Millie here. #Help. #Help me.

"Help me because I NEED help.

"I've decided I want to vlog about friendship and relationships and everything and then I'm NEVER vlogging again. And this time, I'm going to be totally honest with you.

"The fact is, I feel like a liar. I'm giving all this advice and I can't get my own life sorted.

"I'm all glow-y online but offline I'm a massive scribble of manky-la. Here's what happened today. Basically, I was meant to be acting like a Victorian match girl for my aunty Teresa's ghost tour. And while I'm dressed like that, I see ... someone

I really like, and instead of saying something GOOD, I start talking about Canadian ELKS. WHY? WHY? WHY? It's like my brain left my body.

"But on here, I pretend I know stuff and that I'm the one that can give YOU advice. I can't! I mess almost everything up. And not just boys but …

"The IMPORTANT STUFF.

"I know some of you know me or sort of know me. But do you? And do I really know me? The thing is, and please don't think I'm not grateful for all your feedback, I'm spending so much time thinking about this and what I'm going to do on this vlog that I'm missing things in front of me. I'm sorry. This sounds so twonk. And yes, this is a bit of a meltdown but I have someone in my life I've let down so badly. Not by failing to be scary on a ghost tour or by talking about Canadian mammals to a boy I like. I've been ignoring someone who really, REALLY needs me. AND someone who really likes me. And I've been … well, I haven't been fair.

"I have someone in my life who has parents who aren't bad but they are useless. Anyway, she's always been there for me but when I needed to put her first, I didn't. Whereas she's been there for me in EVERYTHING. From the time I got really worried about earthquakes to every test and exam we've ever done at school, when I always think I've done badly. I know I'm sensible but I'm also a very annoying worrier. You can be both at the same time. Sometimes, one leads to another. The more you know, the more scary the world is.

"BUT ANYWAY…

"Anyway, the point is, I didn't give her enough time because of THIS. My vlog. You. And you are magnificent. You are lovely. I can't say that enough. You're not the problem. It's me. It's simple. I need to just make sure I don't miss out on people and actual life. I know, I KNOW, I sound like my mum. I probably sound like your mum too and seriously, I'm not giving a lecture here and neither am I saying I'm giving this up for good. I'm not. I LOVE doing this. I'm just putting life in the right order for now. The order that I think it should be...

"And SEE, this is the real me.

"And I want to say sorry to a person I hope is watching this."

(I get a bit teary at this point.)

"So this is #Help over and out. I'll see you again sometime. Just please know that I haven't got all the answers and I get a lot of stuff wrong. I'm off to put it right now. Well, in the morning. It's late now and my cat needs flea treatment. Not glamorous but fact. Bye."

I upload it. This is probably leaving myself very open to lots of things. But I want Lauren to see it. And I want everyone to know I've messed up.

I pick Dave up and go back to the house. Teresa and Dad are working out the new route for the ghost tour. They're thinking of avoiding the posh flats altogether and using mainly graveyards instead. I hear Grandad saying, "The good thing about dead people is they can't disrupt your ghost tour and, even if they do, that would be a blessing."

Grandad should vlog. He's definitely the most sensible person in this house.

Just as I'm about to put my head on the pillow, I get a notification that Mr Style Shame has posted a photo. When I go to his account, I can't believe what I see.

It's a photo of me as a ghost. I look awful. The filter makes me look even worse. I don't know why Mr Style Shame hates me and Loz so much at the moment. I've done NOTHING to him. He must be a dreadful sexist pig.

I read what he's written.

Talk about #WashedOut. This far from Halloween, the ghost look is NOT attractive #FrightNight #MrStyleShame

How would Mr Style Shame have seen me? There was hardly anyone there. Just a bunch of tourists, Danny and Erin and—

ERIN.

And FINALLY, I realize Mr Style Shame is ERIN. All this time, pretending to be so positive and mindful and wonderful. In reality, she's just a troll with a really big following. She pretends to be a boy but it's her. It MUST be her. She MUST be stopped.

I comment underneath:

It's me in this photo @MilliePorter. I KNOW who you are "MR" Style Shame. You've made it obvious. You need to stop this NOW. Or I am going to tell everyone EXACTLY who you are and EXACTLY what you're about.

I lie back on my pillow and think this is the bravest thing I have ever done. I don't care any more. I've had the worst day EVER. Let Erin say and do what she likes.

I MUST sleep.

#SUPERSTAR

My phone goes off at 6.55 a.m. I've put it under my pillow and the vibrating wakes me up. It's Lauren and she's crying. "I'm SO sorry," she wails.

"No, I'm really sorry," I say. And I've never meant anything more. I am.

"I saw the vlog last night, Millie. I wanted to come round immediately but Dad wouldn't let me. I'm so sorry."

"No! It's me!" I shout. "I'm sorry!"

And Lauren and me say sorry for the next five minutes because we both are, even though my "sorry" is more important than hers.

Lauren then starts giggling. "It's weird, isn't it? You did that vlog and it was really just for me. And yet it's gone viral and everyone in the world has seen it. I could tell you hadn't planned it. It was perfect. An apology, some good advice and COMEDY GOLD!"

I nearly choke on my tongue. "What?!"

"It's gone viral, Millie! Didn't you watch it before you uploaded it?"

"No!" I shout. "It said everything I wanted to and I didn't care!

I just wanted to make a point about you. I actually, GENUINELY, wasn't thinking about shares or likes or subscribers."

"Go and watch it, Millie. It's really funny – like properly hilarious."

"It's not meant to be funny." I feel quite offended.

"But it is," Lauren replies. "It's EPIC!"

I hang up and watch the vlog. I see a very upset and clearly emotional me saying things I really mean but I do sound a bit like a teacher. I'm also so involved in what I'm saying that I completely fail to notice Dave, who has slinked up behind me and spotted Grandad's wading bird calendar lying on the bench.

Dave doesn't like birds. And she really doesn't like ringed plovers. Even paper ones.

When she spots the ringed plover, Dave decides to lift herself up on two legs and dance hypnotically from side to side. She's better than the "'Thriller'' cat and she looks like she's been trained by the world's best choreographers. She then starts diving up and down on top of the plover, licking, head-butting it and twizzling her bum on it.

Someone has relabelled the video – "INSANE cat goes mad behind seriously upset girl". That version has over 75,362 views already.

There are loads of comments. Mostly about Dave.

Cat is EVERYTHING

Need Dave. NOW.

Sat in my pyjamas. School starts in 4 hours. Worth it...

Fake

THAT CAT IS INSANE

Get cat on Strictly. Want to see her samba and Argentine tango

Cat needs own channel

Like if you're watching this when you should be asleep! (612 likes.)

Like if you're watching this and you'd like to lose 10kgs on the Guava Diet! (No likes.)

Finally, I've gone viral.

For potentially all the wrong reasons, but it's actually very sweet that some people enjoyed the message and not the sight of a cat doing the rumba while attacking something that looks like it's wearing a feathery balaclava. So maybe Dave's gone viral and I've—

Wait. I've also got …

5,680 new subscribers!

I scream. Teresa rushes in and wants to know what's happening. I tell her I've gone viral. Teresa opens up the window and shouts, "MILLIE IS VIRAL. HEAR HER!"

Grandad yells, "Is it contagious?! I can't risk it. I had shingles two years ago."

The postman shouts, "I'm thrilled but I can't deliver with this cat threatening me. There are laws against this, you know."

Me and Teresa jump up and down on the bed for a few minutes, then reality slaps me.

Me going viral will lead to the following problems:

- TOTAL laughs at my expense. I'll never be able to move on from this and it will become legendary.

- Danny deciding that I'm just about the worst example of girlfriend material that there could ever be.

- Grandad going mad that Dave has trashed his calendar.
- Mum thinking that something terrible is about to happen to me.
- Erin…

Erin. I check Mr Style Shame.

The entire account has been deleted.

It must have been Erin! I saw right through her and she went for the safe self-destruct option. I can't quite believe it.

My phone vibrates again.

It's Bradley. He doesn't even say hello.

"You know what you need to do, don't you?" he almost yells. Enthusiasm (except for lifts) is unheard of in Bradley.

"Yes. I'm thinking of moving to Paraguay and changing my name."

"I don't think that's necessary. All you need to do is make a vlog called Cats Happen, where you explain that life, like mad cats called Dave, is completely unpredictable and that you've got to roll with it and not worry too much. You can still give great advice. Get Dave in on it. I think it would be really funny. Laugh with the people laughing at you, Mills, and BUILD ON IT."

"Oh, because that's so easy to do – especially with Dave the biggest cat diva ever!" I say. Bradley gets my inner sarcasm like no one else.

"No," he replies. "It's not easy but it's the right thing. Seriously. The video is really funny and you know what? You are…"

And I can hear Bradley really thinking about what he's going to say.

"You are really cool in it, and kind. And if you read all the comments, it's not just about Dave. It's about how you sound like a genuinely lovely person."

When I start groaning loudly, Bradley shuts me up. "No – you do! You do! Seriously Millie, this is a real opportunity now. Everyone will be wondering what you'll do next. So do something brilliant. Make people realize how special you are."

At that moment, I can sense that Bradley feels like he may have gone a bit too far.

"Anyway," Bradley says, "just do it and see what happens. See you soon. Bye superstar!"

And Bradley is right. I need to swallow the feeling inside of me that I just want to escape by paddling to Paraguay on an inflatable novelty doughnut (Teresa has one) and do the vlog to end all vlogs instead. But what do I do about Bradley? I don't want to hurt his feelings, but I think I really fancy—

Danny. No, Bradley's not Danny, but Danny's calling me…

"Lady Viral Sensation! How's life?"

(What is it with men not saying hello today?)

"It's interesting," I say calmly. "I've been totally upstaged by a cat."

"The world loves it. I love it. I think you and Dave are both quirky in that really good British way that's actually sort of Canadian really."

I'm feeling the patriotic sass-ness. "Didn't we have it first, as we did technically invent you?"

Danny pauses. "OK – well, it's probably the Chinese bit of you. OR the French part of you that's the really cool bit – La Millie-Millait." He says it like a really sexy French boy.

I have no idea what he means, so I just say, *"Bon"*, which, apart from *"le stylo"* and *"la chaise"*, is the only French word I can remember.

"Why I'm calling," Danny sort of stutters, "is, would you like to meet me and talk about whatever YOU want to talk about?"

Things have officially got BIG. SERIOUS. MASSIVE. SCARY.

"What about Erin?"

"We've been hanging out a bit," Danny says and he sounds like he's telling the truth. "When I first met her, I thought she was really friendly and cute, but she's got hidden depths – the way a rattlesnake has."

That's what I love about Danny. He's Canadian and naturally knows lots about dangerous exotic animals.

Danny carries on. "But I wanted you to know that Erin told me last night that she runs Mr Style Shame. I saw your comment. You guessed correctly. After that match girl post last night, I pretty much knew it could only be her. It was dumb of her really. Honestly, I don't really want to be associated with someone who runs an account like that. I just think it's nasty. She's got a really nasty streak. I don't like that. And her Instagram was a bit much as well. Not that I'm Mr Gorgeous in those posts or anything. You know she was jealous of you because she knows I think you're funny and … cute."

I don't say anything. I can't quite believe all this is happening.

"Anyway," Danny says nervously, "would you like to do something at the weekend? Say, on Saturday afternoon? We could get ice cream from that little Italian place on the high street? I read a great blog about it."

I surprise myself by what I say.

"Danny, that sounds lovely. I'd really like to, but I've just got to sort a couple of things out first. Can I message you later about it?"

"Sure," he says. "Speak to you in a bit."

I feel sensible again. I feel like I just need … time. Time to work this all out.

I take a big breath. I have to get ready for school or I'm going to be really late, but I also want to see what Erin has posted on HER account, recently. Yes, I know! I should get over it but I can't…

Erin's most recent post is an Instagram photo of her in kitten ears. AGAIN.

These are the sort of cats I like. They don't shed hair everywhere. They're easily controlled and they make you look really cute.

She hasn't got that many likes. People must have realized that SHE was the person making their fashion lives HELL. If they don't, everyone will know at school in about two hours.

I think a non-human may have finally beaten Erin. Dave the cat. YouTube superstar. Rebel. Icon. Mess-maker. SLAYER OF THE BREELER.

I'm not stupid. Erin will be back and probably worse than ever. This is real life, and real life is complicated. Bad girls sometimes win but … I think I've won this part of the war. Well, technically Dave has but I'm her commander in chief.

#IRL

When the history of our time is written, they might call this the greatest Friday ever. Everyone was giving Erin massive evils. There's even a new phrase at school – the Evil Erin. It means you MAJOR death-stare someone and make them feel AWFUL. But I'm trying to be realistic. Everyone knows she's Mr Style Shame, but she's still gorgeous. People will eventually forgive her and she'll be back.

I don't care. Me and Lauren are tight as AND people think my cat is seriously cool. And, I think, because of what's been said at school today, Dave and me need to do one FINAL vlog. If only I could find her.

On my way to the shed after school, Grandad tackles me. "I've noticed, Millie, you spend a huge amount of time getting the perfect self-photograph or the perfect 'vog' while time is passing you by. Have you tried actually sitting with people and talking to them face to face?"

"That's life now!" I tell Grandad gently. "And it's *selfie* and *VLOG*."

"Whatever," Grandad snaps. "But I hope you also realize that life is happening now. Real life." And he pokes me in the shoulder. "Put your phone down – it's not the be-all and end-all of the universe. Another thing: boys aren't always playing games. They're confused too, you know. And don't go full on. Leave some mystery."

This is part of the lecture I've heard Grandad give many times to Teresa. It's his speech from the last century. The best thing to do is nod and say, "Yes!"

He may have a point about the phone though. But I can think about that after I've done my vlog.

"And I'm not happy with my ripped-up calendar, Millie, but I suppose I will just have to live with it."

"Sorry, Grandad," I say and bow my head. He's right. A destroyed plover is a slightly tragic thing to see. "I'll buy you a new one for Christmas."

When I open the shed door, Dave appears from nowhere and darts her way in. It's like she's a celebrity and she knows it.

I sit on the big chair and Dave dives into the space next to me. She curls her legs around the front of her body and sits quietly in front of the camera. Feeling a mixture of brave, sick, terrified and excited, I start filming.

"Hello! It's me, Millie, and this is Dave and, yes, I have kept her in shot this time.

"So, obviously, lots of you saw the video and lots of you are still seeing the video where I'm trying to make a serious point about looking after your friends and Dave – her name is Dave, by the way – decided to freak out in the background and try to kill my grandad's calendar.

"I was, as you can imagine, feeling totally embarrassed and was genuinely thinking about moving abroad and changing my name ... until I realized that YouTube is global anyway. Plus, I can't do that because I have a family who love me loads, despite them being completely insane, and they would miss me. As would my lovely friends, including my brilliant friend Bradley. Do go and have a look at his vlog about escalators. I KNOW it doesn't sound cool but you may actually really come to appreciate them. I sort of have. It was him who said I should just get back on here and say, 'Look – you can't tell cats what to do.' And this is my advice about cats and life in general. You can't control any of it and that's really, really scary. So what you have to do is just let mad cats and mad life do their thing and go with it. You've got no control.

"Remember the very first vlog I did? It's just the same thing.

"For example –" and I look at Dave and command – "Dave, attack the bird!"

(Dave does nothing.)

"Dave, go on two legs and pretend you're in a TV dance competition!"

(Dave does nothing.)

"You see. No control. So this is me, Millie Porter – stress-head, Queen of Sensible, control freak – in charge of a completely unpredictable, uncontrollable life and cat, saying try to chill out as much as you can. Even if you own a mad feline. Bye! #Help me out of here FOR EVER!"

Dave still does nothing.

I upload and feel sort of good about things.

As I message Danny to say I'll meet him on Saturday, Dave starts to act oddly. Typical. When I need her to act calm, she acts strangely.

I suddenly notice that Mum is staring in at the shed's tiny window. She sees me looking, storms in and grabs hold of my hand.

"Mills, I've got something to tell you and it's very important."

#REVELATION

The terrible part of me wants it to be that she's split up with the Neat Freak. The thing about love is, it makes you just a little bit mad and Mum should know. Love has condemned her to a life of bleach – but there are worse things, I suppose. I keep all those bad feelings to myself.

"No – I've haven't split up with Gary."

Why can she always mind-read me with such total rightness?!

"No. It's about my head. You see, Millie, your head is like mine so I know what's going on with it."

Parents are very worrying when they say things like this because they almost certainly have no idea how you're feeling and how your brain is working.

Mum can sense my doubts. "No, really, I can. We've got the same brain. And the brilliant thing about our brain is, it's clever, it makes good decisions – which seems boring now but I promise won't be boring when you're thirty-eight."

Even I don't care about being thirty-eight but I go with it.

"I want to tell you about me and the trees."

I am seriously worried.

"The thing is," Mum continues, "when I was little, there was this outbreak that was killing loads of trees. It was called Dutch elm disease. And I totally got it into my head that Dutch elm disease could spread to humans."

I don't want to sound insensitive. "Mum, where is this going?"

"Listen!" she says, sounding very irritated. "I got myself into a total state. All these trees were dying and there was no Internet. You couldn't just google things. You had to go to the library and... Anyway, so I thought I was dying. With the trees."

I'm confused.

"So, you're saying you were green and environmentally friendly before most other people?"

"No, Millie. I'm saying I was worried about things and got anxiety like you get. I had it. We didn't call it anxiety then. It was called … just being pathetic. But it wasn't. And your brain, I can see, has the same thing. A lot of people have it. Usually, very clever people who are connected and level-headed and…"

"Preach, Mum. Preach," I say – a bit sarcastically, I have to admit.

"No, I need you to really listen, Millie."

And I can see Mum is tearing up a bit, so I shut up.

"When you've got a brain like that, you have to learn to look after it and train it. And you don't have to pretend to be strong when you aren't feeling strong. It's fine to say, 'I don't know what to do.' It's fine to say, 'I can't cope.' It's fine to say, 'I've started this brilliant vlog –' and, Millie, it is great by the way – 'but I don't know the answer to every question and, right now, I just need to keep MY head together.'"

"Did you say that?" This is a major revelation.

"No." Mum looks down. "And I paid for it. I ended up being very poorly. I was in hospital. With this…" Mum taps her head.

It's so odd! I have never ever thought my mum could be the sort of person who would be mentally ill. In a silly way, I thought she was a bit barking for going out with Gary the Neat Freak, but not THIS.

"Mum, I'm so sorry. Why didn't you tell me?"

"You're clever and sensible, Millie, but you don't give children more than they can cope with. It's not fair. When your dad and I split up, we were very sure that both of us were going to make it as easy for you as possible. So you never saw the time I threw an entire packet of premium pork, cider and apple sausages at him." Mum laughs. "It's funny now," she giggles. "It wasn't funny then."

Why do adults always throw groceries at each other? Wet sponges would be a wiser option.

"You're a beautiful, clever, brilliant girl. It's lovely that you want to help people and just give people some of you because you're wonderful. I'm not saying stop doing it – what I'm saying is, you don't have to fix people. It's your job to look after your head and not bring anyone else down. That's all. Anything else is a bonus."

After all this, there's one question that is mainly in the front of my head.

"Can you get Dutch elm disease?"

"No." Mum shakes her head. "But you can get splinters from trying to cuddle trees better. And yes, I did. And yes, I recycle. And that's why my car is electric. You find your little ways to make things … better. Because I still watch the news and think … well… There's always been what you would call spoons, Millie. Spoons in your life and spoons on the news and you—"

"I get it, Mum." I look at her. This has been a major lecture session but it's actually helped a bit.

"Mum, if you ever want to talk about what happened—"

Mum interrupts and goes all hard-faced. "Millie, I don't. It happened. I got through it. And look at me now. A lovely daughter –" she gets hold of me and hugs me – "and a great job and a man who DOES THE HOOVERING."

I shake my head. Mum knows what I'm thinking. "Believe you me, Millie, I know Gary seems like a pain but a kind man who enjoys the feel of a dustpan and brush, sends you flowers all the time and makes you laugh is a pretty good man. But that's a chat for another time. Men are wonderful but they're not the solution. Or women – you may be a lesbian. Which is fine, by the way."

By this stage, it's beginning to feel like I'm listening to a really uncomfortable speech that Mum has planned for years and years.

She gives me a hug. I'm proud. And then she pinches my arm. "All I am saying is, just don't be afraid to ask for help or forget the people who are around you. I'm not saying the people on there –" and her finger slams on the glass screen of my phone a little too hard for my liking – "aren't lovely – but can they do this?!"

And mum gets me in this incredible boa-constrictor-squeeze-hold cuddle, which is both lovely and slightly scary at the same time.

While she is holding me tight, I squeak, "Mum. Can I come home? I'll try to keep things tidy for Gary."

Mum pulls away and says, "Whenever you want, Millie. In my eyes, you NEVER left. And I think it will be better this time. You can have the wireless on till 10 p.m. And I've already had a proper chat with Gary about McWhirter. It's your home too and he has to get used to your crumbs. And from now on, I'll try and make Thursday night Mum-and-Millie night."

We have a little cry until Mum wiggles her head from side to side, does a big sniff and says, "Now, Millie Porter – #helper or whatever you call yourself! – I need to go and have dinner with my boyfriend, who is taking me to the cinema tonight in GOLD class! You get wine and food too. My days of popcorn and half a vat of Diet Coke are gone. Tell you what – if you want to work out what a good man is, find someone who really thinks about YOU rather than what they'd like to do. Goodbye. I love you. And remember I'm here –" and she thumps my hand against her heart – "ANY TIME you want me."

I give my mum another HUGE cuddle and thank her. I don't ask what I really want to ask though.

#MANQUESTIONS

I want to ask Mum about men. Just thinking about them is largely very confusing indeed.

I know Bradley likes me. In fact, I think I now have two boys who like me. But how do you tell one of them that actually you want to be with someone else? I don't want to leave the heart of the other one slightly smashed. Won't I end up feeling dreadful about it ALL? Won't he feel awful?

But I have to do something. Lauren was right. I have been a bit awful about it all.

I wait till Saturday morning and then I message Bradley.

Do you want to meet up?

Bradley replies like he has been sitting on his iPhone.

If you can fit me in global celebrity. See you at 2 at the mall.

I look at my vlog. Loads of views already and it's only been up for half an hour. People must be looking at it as soon as they get notifications. This is great but...

Aunty Teresa comes in and tells me that, with my dad's help, she's finally got her ice-cream van finished and she's thinking of rebranding it as "Ice Scream" and using it as part of her new "nowhere near the posh flats" ghost tour.

This is actually a great idea but I still can't think of anything but Bradley. I'm really nervous.

When I get to the shopping centre, the clock moves as slowly as Dave the cat when you want her to do something, and then finally, eventually...

It's 2 p.m. and 43 seconds.

I see Bradley. He's never late.

In almost-silence, Bradley and I go and sit down on his favourite bench between his favourite lift and the double-fronted Otis lift that secretly goes to the basement if you press the right buttons.

I look at him and stutter, "Bradley ... I really like you..."

"I know," he says. "But you really, REALLY like Danny. Mr Normal. And I suppose he doesn't bore you with lifts. And escalators."

"Actually, Bradley –" I stare at him intently – "I want you to know I do have a new-found respect for lifts that I never had before I met you. I like to think if I can open my mind up to the gift of engineering, then..."

Bradley looks gutted.

"Don't tell me – you should never have kissed me."

"No, I shouldn't," I whisper. I'm a cow.

"Don't worry." Bradley sighs sarcastically. "What girl can resist my geek talk? And now I suppose you just want to be friends."

This is awful. I cannot describe how terrible I feel. I would HATE it if someone did this to me.

"Please can we?" I whisper.

"No," Bradley snaps. Then he becomes gentler. "No. No. No. It doesn't work like that. Because right now I want to be horrible to you and say the worst things ever, and, seriously, I just need to go before I say something, because … I just need to go."

Bradley disappears in a Sigma Solon Mid-Rise lift (he's taught me a lot). As I look back, the doors shut behind him really slowly. You can't slam a lift. That's the problem.

Horrible. Horrible. Horrible.

That's how I feel.

I call Mum and explain. I just need some advice right now.

"Did you mean to hurt him?" Mum asks.

"Of course not!" I shout.

"But you still did, Millie, and that's life. He'll be OK after a while. Male pride is a very complicated thing. In fact, ANY pride is a very complicated thing. You're going to hurt people and people are going to hurt you. But you can't live a lie. Look at Lauren's parents. Hearts rule where heads fear to tread, Millie. Get used to it."

In the middle of the shopping centre, I ask Mum a very important question: "Mum, does this get easier?"

"Oh no!" Mum says and she's brutal. And then she corrects herself. "Yes, it does, darling. You learn to manage it a bit better. And you can see the problems galloping down the road before they knock you over. Usually. Not always. But here's a tip – don't you DARE share what happened with that boy ANYWHERE. No vlog. No Facebooking, or whatever it's called. Some things, Millie, are not and never will be for public consumption. Sharing YOUR thoughts is one thing. Sharing the pain of others without their permission is just cruel. DO NOT do it. You're not my Millie, the girl I know and love, if you do."

I know she's right. Even though it would make the best subject matter ever for a vlog.

"Don't worry, Millie. Bradley will find someone else. And then YOU'LL be jealous and wonder what's happening. You'll ask yourself 'Have I made the right decision?' But I hope you'll be happy that such a lovely young man, and he sounds like one, has found happiness."

And I will be – it's just that…

When I started this whole thing, I thought I knew loads. But it's been by sharing what I thought was lots that I've realized that I've got quite big gaps of things I have no clue about. Although escalators now aren't one of them.

Life is very confusing. Or, as Grandad says when he's trying to sound very clever indeed, this whole thing seems to have led to a great deal of "confusement".

Now I've just got to wait around for Danny. Two boys in one day. I feel a bit of a cow and I hope Erin isn't around. I hope no one's around. I might go and hide in Debenhams.

#DANNY

I see Danny floating towards me, and honestly, I know I've made the right decision. Don't hate me. I know it's shallow, but he's GORGEOUS.

"Hello, my lady of global fame. How are you?"

"Well. Not really global fame. But. Yes. Doing quite well vlogging-wise. I'm good. I wondered…"

"Yes," he says. "The answer is yes. I would love to buy you an ice cream."

What follows is a stupendous kiss. It's the equivalent of a million likes on every platform ever. A mass of emoticons and hearts and a huge THUMBS ALOFT firework that sends me off my head. Do they teach kissing in schools in Ontario? I think they must do and Danny must have passed with the best grade possible.

It's a kiss that makes me feel brave and brilliant and…

"Danny. I really like you."

We kiss AGAIN. This is truly magnificent.

"I really like you too, Miss Porter, Problem Sorter. Can I take you to Wagamama's this evening?"

I would love to go and slurp noodles with Danny. But I have

to be honest. "I'd love to, Danny. But I can only hang out this afternoon, because there's something really important I've got to do this evening."

Danny looks disappointed.

"Look. I'm thinking you want to sort of try the 'be my boyfriend' thing?"

Danny smiles. "Yeah."

"Well, me too. I mean, I want to be your girlfriend but—"

Danny interrupts. "But you'll have lots of options now you're a global sensation."

This takes me totally by surprise. "Oh no! It's not that. The thing about vlogging is, it's wonderful but … I just want to enjoy people I can actually poke in the arm!"

I jab Danny's bicep. He must work out because it's hard, but he pretends it hurts.

"I've just learnt that to be a great vlogger, I've also got to— I wanted to be famous and I tried a bit too hard and then, when Dave did what she did, it just proved—"

"It proved what?" Danny asks me.

"I'm not sure." This makes us both laugh.

"Look, can we do something tomorrow instead?" I ask him. "Maybe the cinema? I'll message you. There's just something I've got to do and it's important I do it tonight."

I can see Danny still looks hurt, so I tell the truth. "It's not vlogging or anything. It's family. Do you know what I mean?"

Danny grins and winks. "I know exactly what you mean. I'm away from a lot of mine and I miss them. You want to make sure you spend time with them."

"That's just it!" I say.

Danny and me then have another terrific kiss. When I open my eyes, two beautiful pools of lovely are smiling back at me.

Sorry. Vomfest. But the boy is magical.

"Message me," he whispers and blows a kiss.

It's hard to leave such a hero of pure beauty.

But there's someone I really need to spend time with.

#GIRLTIME

"Mills, HOW DID IT GO?!" Lauren screams down the phone. "I've been sitting here actually feeling sick. What happened? What did they say? Was it basically *Hollyoaks*?"

Lauren sounds as if she's about to explode. I'm at Mum's and feeling more chilled.

"l wondered if you wanted to come round tonight and eat pizza and try to get Dave to do tricks for pepperoni?"

"For your vlog?" she asks.

"No. Just for us," I say. "The sisters in crime, talking in rhyme…"

Lauren picks up our rap that we made up when we were eight: "Don't eat lime. Don't taste fine."

We both finish it together: "Give up talking. Just do a little mime."

It's RUBBISH but it's our theme song and we start giggling a lot.

"Can I come round now?" Lauren asks. "My mum's back and it's like a war zone again."

I tell her that I'll see her in ten minutes.

While I'm waiting for Lauren, I look at the comments on my latest vlog and nearly drop dead.

Enjoyed this book? Tweet us your thoughts.

#Help   @RaeEarl   @WalkerBooksUK

ABOUT THE AUTHOR

RAE EARL was born in Stamford, Lincolnshire in 1971. After some adequate schooling, she went to Hull University and won the Phillip Larkin prize for a frankly magnificent essay. She then did every job possible at a radio station. Her books *My Mad Fat Diary* and *My Madder Fatter Diary*, which are based on her own teenage diaries, have been made into a TV show that is aired in over 50 countries. It has been nominated for 2 BAFTAS and 2 RTS awards and won 2 MIND Media awards. She is also the author of the OMG! series of books. Rae lives in Hobart, Australia, where she is currently writing, among other things, a TV drama about a girls' football team.

@RaeEarl

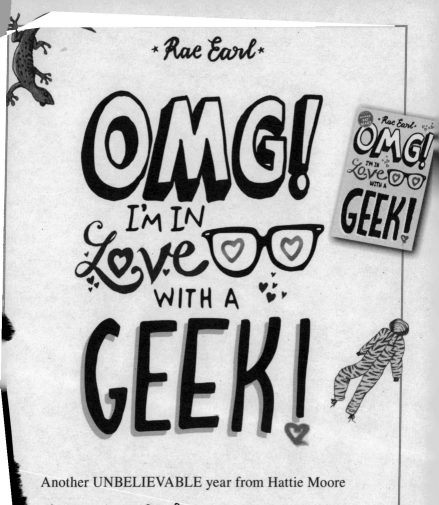

Rae Earl

OMG!
I'M IN
Love
WITH A
GEEK!

Another UNBELIEVABLE year from Hattie Moore

This year I will find full-on, long-term love. And it DEFINITELY won't be with Goose who lives next door. I will also take it upon myself to help Gran with her iPad so she doesn't end up global laughing stock. And finally, I will officially get to know my real dad. This year is going to be totally AMAZEBALLS!

* Rae Earl *

OMG!

is this

ACTUALLY

my Life?

An UNBELIEVABLE year from Hattie Moore

I'm totally telling you that this year, I'm going to find my real dad! Can you EVEN believe I don't know who he actually is? I won't be stopped by my family or the evil dog that lives 3 doors away. And another thing, with the help of Dimple and Weirdo Jen, I will become a TOTAL hotness goddess and defeat the dark forces of Miss Gorgeous Knickers and her gang. I tell you, this is going to be the most OMG year EVER!

ACKNOWLEDGEMENTS

Thank you, as ever, to the usual suspects with special love to the legendary Jordana 'Retainer Linda Hamilton alike' Green, Jo-Anne Green and Gracie Upton.

Lenah Valley Post Office for ever...

Hello, Millie. You can see by my verified account that I represent some of this country's biggest vloggers. I'd be interested in talking to you. And your cat. I think you are both wonderful. Thanks. Lydia Portancia

This is BIG. Really BIG. I mean, we're talking someone who could really take me on. Move things forward. Someone who…

Someone who can wait.

Tonight is about my best friend. We'll discuss it later. Perhaps. For the moment, everything can wait. I need major spoon time with the Loz.

I think the key to a sensible life is just putting all the cutlery in the right spaces and using each piece at the right time. Don't you?

That and having a cat that doesn't think she's a trapeze artist. I can see Dave walking along the washing line, and every so often, swinging round it. And no, I'm not filming it. Not now. But maybe check my vlog later…